The SEA BEAST
TAKES a lover

Michael Andreasen is a graduate of the
University of California, Irvine's MFA
program. His fiction has appeared in *The
New Yorker*, *Tin House*, *Zoetrope: All-
Story*, *Quarterly West*, and elsewhere. He
lives in Southern California. *The Sea Beast
Takes a Lover* is his first book.

The SEA BEAST TAKES a lover

MICHAEL ANDREASEN

HEAD
OF ZEUS

An Apollo Book

This is an Apollo book. First published in the UK in 2018 by Head of Zeus Ltd
This paperback edition first published in the UK in 2018 by Head of Zeus Ltd

9 7 5 3 1 2 4 6 8

A catalogue record for this book is available from the British Library.

ISBN (PB): 9781788545990
ISBN (E): 9781786696625

Set in Rotation LT
Designed by Nancy Resnick

Printed and bound by CPI Group (UK) Ltd, Croydon, CR0 4YY

Head of Zeus Ltd
First Floor East
5–8 Hardwick Street
London EC1R 4RG

WWW.HEADOFZEUS.COM

For my parents

Contents

The SEA BEAST
TAKES a lover

Our Fathers at Sea

The night before we load you into the crate and watch as the helicopter carries you off to the undisclosed location to drop you into the Atlantic Ocean, we eat dinner as a family. I roll your wheelchair to the head of the table, which has always been a little too small for five, so that it's clear to everyone who's being honored. I'd hoped to grill up a few of those rib eyes we've got in the garage freezer—it seemed the right occasion for it—but then Avery recalled how you'd always loved Rosemary's braised chicken back when you were still on solid food, and so, in honor of you, even though you aren't eating, that's what we eat.

We try conversation for a little while. I think about going around the table and having everyone share their favorite memories with Grandpa, but I know in order to do that I'll need a really good memory, which I don't know if I have. As I try to come up with something, Ernest turns on the little TV we keep on the kitchen counter. I assume Rosemary will object, but she's busy checking the drip on your IV and I'm busy remembering, so we let it go.

As we eat we watch *Little Winston*, part of the whole-some black-and-white hour of family programming that usu-ally rounds out our dinnertime. They're airing the Father's Day episode, which we've seen a hundred times, but I think we all realize the importance of watching it again today, especially for the boys.

Little Winston and his father, Big Al, sit on the front stoop of Big Al's Gas 'n Fixit. They've just returned from watching Chester, Big Al's father and Little Winston's grandfather, get crated away. Their untouched glasses of lemonade sweat in the afternoon heat. Little Winston is folding and unfolding his sausagey fingers on the lap of his blue overalls, which he always does when he's upset, and Big Al is trying to con-sole him.

"It makes me scared," Little Winston says, tears poised to roll on the edges of his cheeks, "to think that one day they'll carry you off in one of those big crates, Big Al. That one day they'll drop you into the sea at the undisclosed location with a bunch of strangers. That I'll never see you again."

"I know, son," Big Al says. His thick mechanic's arms, normally crossed over his grimy blue work shirt in stoic dis-approval of Little Winston's comic hijinks, are now on the boy's shoulders, his rough, greasy hands straightening Win-ston's cowlicked hair in one of the series' rare moments of paternal tenderness. "When you get to be my age, you'll understand."

"I'm not gonna be able to do it, Big Al," Little Winston sniffs. "I'm not gonna know when or how."

"You will," Big Al assures him, his hand on the boy's back. "You will. Just follow your heart."

"I love you," Little Winston mutters.

"Just follow your heart," says Big Al. "That's all I'm doing here."

"I love you, Big Al," Little Winston repeats.

"I love you, too, little buddy," says Big Al. "I love you, too."

Gurdy Bills, the actor who played Little Winston, is an old man now, and kind of a local celebrity. He retired to an enormous house up in the north foothills, and resurfaces from time to time for little events and fund-raisers. I'm always surprised that people still come out to see him, since he never did another show after *Little Winston*. I remember once, not long after we crated Mom, we took you and the kids down to Ainsdale to watch him cut the ribbon on the new Pine Pleasant Mall. It was some crowd.

I ask Rosemary when she expects we'll read they've crated Gurdy Bills. I even smirk a little, thinking this is a bit ironic, considering what we've just watched, and would have enjoyed a brief discussion about how the years catch up with all of us eventually, how we should take the time to savor its fleeting preciousness, etc. I think maybe this is something the boys ought to hear, that the time is right, but Rosemary is in no mood. This episode always makes her well up, and she's especially tearful tonight. She tells Avery to sit on her lap so that she can stroke his downy arm hair and make small, popping kisses against his ear. Avery knows his mother needs him, and though he's old enough to sense that being babied is something he should resist, he doesn't. At the other end of the table, Ernest has gathered the bones from our plates and is attempting to reconstruct the entire chicken.

When Rosemary's done mothering him, Avery asks if he can be excused from the table.

"Kiss your grandfather good night," I say.

"Gross," Ernest says, but Avery understands. He rounds the table to you, leans over the tray of your wheelchair, and kisses your cheek the way he kissed mine back in the days when he used to kiss me, as young boys sometimes do before their fathers put a stop to it. But it means something to me in this moment, watching my son give you, my father, this sincere kiss good-bye, which is why I think you and everyone else will forgive me when I say that he is the good one and, of my two sons, the one I prefer.

Then you start having one of your fits.

It's a shame that Avery is so close, and he's just finished such a sweet thing, such a gentle act of affection, because your fits terrify him. Right away, his chin rumples like a raisin to lock down incoming tears. I try to steady you so that Rosemary can secure the straps to your head and arms. Avery disappears upstairs to cry out of sight, no doubt assuming that his act of love has somehow caused your spasm. You pull against the straps like a weight lifter, drool snaking down your chin in little fingers. As I force your shoulders against the back of the chair, I can't help blaming you a little for ruining what had been a really beautiful moment, because a chance like that doesn't come again, and now

4

Avery, who is already extremely sensitive, will always have this crappy memory attached to kissing his grandfather the night before he was crated.

Hours later, while Rosemary readies the boys for bed, I put a couple bottles of good beer in my coat and wheel you out onto the porch so that we can enjoy the lake at night. It's our lake, yours and mine, and now mine and my sons'. For all the fighting, all the hurt feelings, the years of not talking even before you lost the ability to speak, we still end up here, you and I, looking at a lake full of stars.

For some reason, one of the beers is much warmer than the other, almost room temperature, but rather than spoiling the moment by running back in for another, I suck it up and decide to just drink a warm beer. I put a straw in the colder one and set it on your tray, then lift my warm one and say, "Well, here's to you, Dad. We sure will miss ya."

I take a drink while you let the straw find your mouth. You manage a few sips and seem pleased with them. We look out on the lake, admiring the way its stillness makes everything around it seem not as quiet. I suddenly remember the memory I should have remembered at dinner, the day you taught me to catch tadpoles, which we used to keep in an old mason jar with a few inches of water. You showed me how controlling the water level prevented them from maturing into frogs, and how nice it was to keep tadpoles as they were, blindly swimming around until they died and we replaced them with new ones. It's a practice I've passed on to the boys, who've lived their whole lives with jars of black blobs sitting on their windowsills, never imagining they should grow to be anything more than what they are.

That night I dream that Mom and I are standing on the small dock just beyond the house. She's the age she was when I was in high school, still decades away from crating. She tells me that you died in your sleep. In the dream she calls you "Daddy," which she never did in life. "Daddy's gone," she says, and I feel the relief whistle out of me like an untied balloon. You're gone. I don't have to crate you. I'm so happy I dive into the lake, where the dream lets me breathe freely, the warm water hugging me close until I wake up.

I go to your room to check on you, the way Rosemary will on the boys after she's had a bad dream about them, or a bad feeling, or just wants to know that they're safe. Like you, I've never put much stock in dreams. I'm not checking on you because I think mine has come true, though it would definitely make things easier on everyone.

You have enough blankets to keep you warm, and your IV bag is full and dripping properly thanks to Rosemary, who always puts you to bed, and again I realize how lucky I am to have a wife who treats you like her own. As I get closer I can see that some of the sheets are twisted around you, which means you've been fitting in your sleep. I consider strapping you to the bed for the rest of the night like we sometimes do, but I can always tell from the looks you give me in the morning that you've slept badly, and I don't want to get one of those looks tomorrow, so I leave you be.

I realize now that we could have made the room a little nicer for you. The curtains are old and faded, and there isn't much on the walls except for a print of a sandpiper-ridden beach that's been hanging there since we moved in. It's nothing like the boys' room, which we've always tried to keep comfortable and cheerful to make up for the fact that they share.

The other day I caught Ernest standing in your doorway, sizing up the place. At first I thought he might be mustering the courage to come in and spend some time with you, to talk to you or hold your hand for once in his life, but then I remembered that Rosemary and Avery had taken you for one last stroll on the little boardwalk that circles the water. We've promised Ernest your room after you're gone, but the sight of him mentally replacing your things with his made me uneasy as a parent. Yesterday he showed me a floor plan he'd drawn. He pointed to where his TV will go, and described the loft he wants to build to free up more floor space. Whenever he looks at you now with that cool, unsmiling stare of his, I worry that maybe he isn't turning out the way I'd like him to.

On the dresser are some of your old photos. There's a close-up of Mom when she was the age I am now, and one of you and your brothers as kids on a first day of school. They're too far from the bed for you to see, which means you probably haven't seen them in a while.

I get an idea. I take the photos downstairs and tape them

to the tray of your chair, so that tomorrow in the crate, when you look down, you'll see them, Mom and your family and everyone looking up at you. I add one of you and me from that trip to the Kenner River when I was eleven, just a few months after we crated your dad, which is probably why you planned it. We took our time canoeing the river, with Mom driving ahead each day to lay out a picnic at the spot where we'd break for lunch. The picture, which she must have taken from the shore, is of the two of us on the water, our toes dragging in the lazy current. I also tape down the photo from the mantel that we used for this year's Christmas card. We're at the state fair, huddled around a pumpkin that's shaped like a pig. Sure, Avery's ruining it a little with that ridiculous pig face he's making, but we all seem pretty happy, even you, in your chair with Rosemary's hands clasped around your neck in an adoring way. I head back to bed, but I'm so pleased about the photo idea that it's hard to drift off.

That morning at breakfast Avery gives you a picture he's drawn. It shows a crate, one of the modern titanium models with a wide pressure-resistant window, through which we can see a man waving. Avery says this is you. The crate is set against a background of deep blue, suggesting that it's already been dropped at the undisclosed location. Outside the crate, walking along an ocean floor next to a single starfish and a lone hermit crab, is another figure wearing a kind of space suit, waving back. Avery says this is him. I want to ask him why he didn't draw the crate before the drop, so that we could all be waving together, but for a moment I think the way Rosemary encourages me to think—that is, with patience, with understanding—and I don't ask. Instead I tell him it's a great drawing. I tell him that you like it, though you're not looking at it. You're looking at him, but in a cross-eyed way that I can tell is making him uncomfortable, and I'm mad at you all over again, because this is your chance to make up for last night and you're blowing it.

As we head to the car, Ernest calls shotgun. I tell him we're giving you the front seat today so that you can get a good view of the lake one last time before you leave. He asks if he can have shotgun on the way back. I pretend not to hear him and wheel you around to face the house.

"There's the house, Dad," I say.

It doesn't look great. I've been meaning to repaint, especially the shutters and trim, which have shed pretty much every trace of their original blue. Half the porch balusters are missing, kicked out by Ernest during one tantrum or another. I honestly don't know if you have any sentimental attachment to this place, and suddenly it occurs to me to drive you up to see the old family home in Clark County where you grew up. I don't even know if the house is still there. The drive is forty-five minutes each way, and crating check-in is at eleven on the dot.

Maybe just this house is enough. Maybe you can look at this one and think of the other one. Standing behind the chair, I can't tell where you're looking, so I walk around to check. Rosemary has dressed you in your gray linen suit—baggy at the shoulders and around the waist from all the

9

weight loss—and your bolo tie with the silver deer-skull slider, which is not what I would have chosen, even if it is classic Dad, because I guess I have a greater sense of symbolism than she does, but it's too late now. You're fixed on a patch of goldenrod crawling out from under the porch, staring at it blankly, like if I were to poke you in the eye my finger would just go right through, and while I'm disappointed that you don't seem to be lost in a moment of pleasant reminiscence, at least you're not noticing the second-floor gable, which is sloughing off shingles like it has some kind of disease, or the man-size weeds choking the last bit of life out of the raspberry bushes Rosemary planted a million summers ago.

"Yep," I say. "That's where we lived."

We make it to the mall parking lot just fine, but I've forgotten that there's a Sugar Scoops in this strip, so right away Ernest starts howling for a cone. I tell him there'll be cotton candy and popcorn at the loading site, but even I know that can't compete with Sugar Scoops, where they mix cookie chunks and gummy bears into your ice cream right in front of you. I decide maybe this is just Ernest's way of getting into the spirit of things, of making the day special, so we spend several extra minutes ordering everyone a cone before crossing the baking sheet of black asphalt to the loading site on the other side of the parking lot. I imagine you must be roasting alive in your suit, because I'm roasting alive in mine, but maybe linen breathes better than a cotton-wool blend. Rosemary has mashed some of her ice cream into a soup, which she's feeding you. Strictly speaking, she's not supposed to do this, as it's still technically solid food, but you seem to enjoy it. You look straight at her as she spoons the pink goo between your lips, and you move your mouth in a way that suggests you at least remember how to eat. It's a nice moment for the two of you, so I don't say anything. Instead I find the check-in desk and write your full name and date of birth on the white and yellow forms.

We pass through a sort of plywood gateway into the event area, where we'll wait until the boarding starts. Inside are the cotton candy and popcorn booths, and a guy standing next to a helium tank with a fistful of balloons. Nearby, a portable stereo plays patriotic rock anthems behind a juggler doing five bowling pins at once. At the center of everything is the crate. Through its enormous picture window we can clearly see the three dozen or so empty red velvet seats like the skybox at a baseball stadium. The silver cables riveted to its frame run to a decommissioned military helicopter dozing at the edge of the lot.

I remember when we did this with your dad. The whole thing seemed weightier then, maybe because there was a live brass band instead of a portable stereo, or because in those days we held cratings in city parks and squares instead of mall parking lots, or maybe I was just young and everything adults did seemed bigger and more important. I remember one of the clowns made me a balloon giraffe, and your father asked, like some do, not to be taken, to be held over till the following year. Next year, he promised, he'd be ready. I don't

11

remember what you did, if you wept or tried to argue with him, or if you simply stood by like I am now. I remember that he had the good sense to ask only once, but even that small moment of pleading caught me off guard, and I couldn't shake it for weeks after. When it was time for the helicopter to take off, I couldn't look, afraid I'd see his face through one of the portholes, which at that time were only big enough to show faces and nothing else. Instead I turned to the clown with the balloons, who of course by then wasn't clowning at all. He was watching the helicopter and the crate fade into the distance with everyone else, his makeup and rubber nose unable to hide the fact that, despite knowing no one in the crate, and probably attending events just like this one several times a year, he still felt something strong and meaningful watching it go, and as I watched him watch it, I realized what a sin it was to look away.

I wait with you in the event area while Rosemary takes the boys to get balloons. I'm at least happy to see that people still dress up. All of the adult men are wearing neckties, and it dawns on me now that my powder blue tie with the little crests and coats of arms would have gone well with the suit you're wearing. Better than the bolo, the hollowed-out sockets of the skull reminding us all in the most tasteless way why we're here, which I can't believe Rosemary didn't consider as she was dressing you. "Should he wear the deer-skull slider?" she could have asked me. "You know, the one that makes him look like the worst sort of backwater lake rat? Or do you have something more appropriate to the solemnity of the occasion?" And I would've pulled out the powder blue tie, with its little chevroned shields and rearing lions and fleurs-de-lis, and she would've smiled, and nodded, and noted to herself how fortunate she was to have a husband who understands the importance of detail within the context of greater events.

The two men standing beside us wear burgundy suits and matching ties, like performers in a men's choir. The son is tall and proud, with a steady hand on his father's shoulder. The father's hands shake at his side, but not out of fear. Both his face and his son's are cheerful and calm, plump and pinchred in the cheeks, as if this is exactly the day they'd hoped to see from the moment they woke up. I find myself standing straighter just looking at them, and I ease your shoulders against the back of the wheelchair so that you're slouching a little less.

"Some crate, eh, Pops?" the son says to the father. "Nothing like Granddad's. That thing was just a steel box with metal seats and a few glass portholes, remember? And what about his dad's? Can you believe that once upon a time the crates were actually crates? As in, made out of wood? Not even airtight! Those dads drowned as they sank. Not exactly what I'd call respect for your elders. But harder times, I suppose. This, though—just look at it. Do you have any idea how many psi these reinforced frames can withstand? Boatloads, Pops. Just boatlaods."

The father regards the crate with a satisfied expression, as if to say that, indeed, it is some crate.

"And don't forget the pressure-resistant window," the son adds. "You'll be able to see those dolphins nice and clear.

How about that, Dad? Dolphins all the way down, keeping you company."

I've heard of this—reports of dolphins gathering at the undisclosed location. I want to ask the son privately if this is just something cheerful he's decided to say, or if he has actual evidence of dolphins, if he knows someone who can confirm it.

Regardless, I'm hoping that you heard him. Dolphins, Dad. Maybe whales and anemones, too, and great schools of silvery fish. You're studying Avery's underwater picture, which Rosemary clipped to your tray with the clips we use to hold the newspaper in place when we think that you might like to look at it. I wish that Avery had drawn a few dolphins swimming alongside the crab and the starfish, to give you a better sense of just how comforting this whole business is going to be. Then I remember the photographs under the drawing. I unclip the edge of the paper, and it furls lazily to one side, revealing the shot of you and me in the canoe, our arms and knees sunburned, our chins pointed intrepidly forward. This, I think, is the image you should be contemplating, and I want to point it out to you, to remind you of that day and all that hopefulness, but you're not looking down anymore. Instead, you're looking where everyone else is looking, at a man moving slowly from the check-in desk to the crate, followed by a small assembly of beaming fans.

It's Gurdy Bills. Little Winston himself.

He's balder and rounder than he was in his mall-opening days, but still has the aura of a television personality, the confident walk and eyes. He wears long white robes and carries an old-fashioned sickle in one hand and a baby in the other. The baby, wrapped in its own little toga, is sucking on what looks like an hourglass. The costume is meant to amuse—Gurdy Bills is, after all, a performer, a comedian— and many laugh and applaud what they see. Even the juggler stops to watch.

Rosemary rejoins us with the boys in tow, each holding a balloon and a sky blue plume of cotton candy.

"Isn't that something," she says. "With a baby and everything."

Standing beside Bills is a less bald, less round man wearing blue overalls and a gelled cowlick. We assume this is his son. After handing off the baby, Bills turns to this man, and the two begin a little recital.

"It makes me scared," Bills's son says clearly, cheating his stance to the side and projecting so that everyone can hear him, "to think that one day they'll carry you off in one of those big crates, Dad. That one day they'll drop you into the sea at the undisclosed location with a bunch of strangers. That I'll never see you again."

"I know, son," Gurdy Bills says. His expression is focused and concerned, and in spite of the ridiculous getup, and the fact that we're all standing in the middle of a strip mall parking lot, the scene is suddenly intimate. "When you get to be my age, you'll understand."

"I'm not gonna be able to do it, Dad," Bills's son says. "I'm not gonna know when or how."

"You will," Gurdy Bills says, a hand on his son's overalled back. "You will. Just follow your heart."

15

"I love you," Bills's son says with a smile.

"Just follow your heart," says Bills. "That's all I'm doing here."

"I love you, Dad," Bills's son says. Now he's looking out at all of us.

"I love you, too, little buddy," says Gurdy Bills. "I love you, too."

Everyone cheers. Even Ernest. He's smiling and clapping like it's the best thing he's ever seen. I wonder if we shouldn't take Ernest to see more live theater, maybe a show now and then down at that little dinner theater place in Phillipsburg that Rosemary's always talking about. Maybe it's the sort of thing that would help him locate something different and good inside himself.

Then Gurdy Bills raises a hand, and everyone is quiet.

"We go to see our fathers," he says. "We are not afraid."

And with that, he hugs his son, kisses the baby in the toga and the woman holding him, and climbs the ramp into the crate.

"How about that, Dad?" I say to you. "In the same crate as Gurdy Bills."

The men begin to file into line. Rosemary bends to kiss you on the cheek, then sniffles into a Kleenex. Avery cautiously pets your shoulder, afraid to get too close. Noticing his rolled-up drawing, he gently slips its corners back into their clips, the photographs of the family and our day in the canoe vanishing once again beneath a scribbled ocean. Ernest is looking at you, and while it isn't exactly a loving look—more of a standoffish look, the look of a gunslinger just before he draws—it's the last moment you'll have with him, so I don't want to interfere. Eventually he tucks his sprig of cotton candy, which by now is just a cardboard tube and a few thin wisps of blue sugar, into the space between your stomach and the tray. As I wheel you off, I want to believe—need to believe—that he was sharing the last of it with you and not just throwing it away.

We're at the end of the line because you don't need a seat. There's an alcove for your chair and two others in the front row. While we wait, I try to think of some final thing to say to you.

There isn't enough time to get into the whole money thing, even though I want you to know I don't care about that anymore. I could just say that, just say, "I want you to know, Dad, I'm not sore about the money anymore," but without going into the reasons why I don't care, why I actually stopped caring a long time ago but couldn't say so because I needed you to believe I still cared, it would just sound like I'm letting you off the hook. I could promise that I'll always look after the old family home in Clark County, except, like I said, I'm not sure it's still there. Besides, I want to send you off with something forward-looking. Something hopeful. Through the window, I can see the other sons whispering into their fathers' ears, saying soothing, important things. Some are in tears. Some are burying their faces in their fathers' laps, begging forgiveness for this thing we are about to do, or a worse thing that came before it. Some say nothing. None of the fathers are asking not to be taken, which is rare. Maybe they don't want to embarrass themselves in front of Gurdy Bills, to be the one blubbering and begging while the great actor sits smiling in his white robes, ready for the plunge.

I want to know what Gurdy Bills's son is saying to him. I want to know what you said to your father. I want to tell you not to worry, but I don't think you are worried. I want to tell you not to be afraid, but there's no sign of fear on your face. I can't tell if you're comfortable. I don't know if you're content. You give nothing away.

Nozzle heads hang from the ceiling inside the crate, waiting to release anesthetic gas when you reach critical depth. I wish Avery could see these. I don't know if he knows about them, but he should, to understand that we're not monsters. That we care what happens to you after you drop.

As soon as I ease your chair into the alcove, you start having one of your fits. Your wrists rattle and your head bangs and you make the same little choking sound you always do. I don't have Rosemary to help hold you, and if I strap you down now, you'll stay that way for the entire trip. I try to brace you against the chair, to press my weight against the bucking of your body, hugging you tight as you struggle under me like a trapped animal. You can't break free. I am so much bigger than you.

Over your shoulder I can see the other fathers and the last of the sons staring at us. We're ruining the moment they're collectively trying to have. But what about my moment? Is this the moment they think I wanted? Is this any kind of send-off for a man who has done, if not great things, then at least good things? Things that he didn't have to do, was not required to do, and yet did anyway, decently and with only minimal complaint? Doesn't that deserve its own moment? And yet here I am. This is all I can do.

You stop seizing. I feel something wet on my shoulder. In your fit, you've spit up the ice cream. It's oozing down your chin in waves of thick pink, dribbling onto your shirt and pants. I don't carry a handkerchief. Rosemary usually keeps Kleenex in her purse. I take Avery's drawing off the tray and use it to wipe your face and dab at the little pool in your lap. I can't look you in the eyes. I just dab until the helicopter's copilot tells me he's sealing the doors.

Everyone has been moved to an outer perimeter so that the helicopter can take off safely. It isn't until I see Avery's face that I realize I'm still holding his crumpled pink puke-stained drawing. He's already in a fragile state, and this sends him over the edge. He presses his face into Rosemary's dress so hard and deep there's no way he can breathe. This is an old tactic he used to great effect when he was smaller, until I asked Rosemary to please stop coddling him, because it was plainly making him weak, and although I didn't want a repeat of Ernest, I also didn't want a son who suffocated himself in his mother's skirts. But now she picks him up right away, staring at the soggy paper in my hand like it's a bloody stump.

This is the last thing we need right now. We should be gathering around one another as a family, relying on our shared love and support to light a path out of this parking lot and back to the happy lives we've worked so hard for. Instead, we're a good three feet from one another, except for Avery, who's reburied himself in Rosemary's left breast, gagging on his own tears and shuddering in that baby-mouse way he does. She hands me his balloon like she wants me to go murder myself with it.

"We'll wait in the car," she says, which strikes me as a big mistake. Yes, the drawing thing was also a mistake, but this is so much more important in ways I know Rosemary doesn't see. This could do real, lasting damage to our son.

"If he doesn't see it take off," I say, loud enough so Avery can hear over his muffled caterwauling and the slow build of the helicopter's engines, "he might regret it later."

Rosemary covers his exposed ear with her free hand and says, "What the *hell* do you expect me to do?"

"I just don't want him to regret not doing the right thing when he had the chance," I say, almost shouting now so that he can hear me through her hand.

She resituates Avery on her hip and carries him away as the helicopter separates from the asphalt.

I still have Ernest. I put my hand on his shoulder as the whirring blades make small cyclones of gravel and trash. Everyone shields their eyes, except for you and the others facing us through the glass. The pilot has a practiced hand. The crate lifts slowly as the cables go taut, with only a slight, cradling rock. Once it's high enough, we all release our balloons. Ernest lets go of his, and I let go of Avery's, hoping he's watching from the car as they become a distant flock of color in a far-off sky. Ernest waves to the crate as it rises. We cannot take our eyes off it, but still, I know he and I are looking at two different things. Where I see a crate carrying my father away, and someday me if I'm lucky, Ernest sees only the resettling of dust, the spinning of rotors, and the might of engines bearing the weight of what is necessary.

I'm not sure what to do, Dad. It's all I can think standing here with Ernest, watching you go. I surprise myself by saying it out loud.

"I'm not sure what to do."

It comes out like a cry, the roaring of the helicopter still knocking around inside my ears.

"Just wave, Dad," Ernest says, as though it were the easiest thing in the world. And so I do. And it is easy.

In a few minutes, after the crate shrinks to the size of a punctuation mark, I will uncrumple Avery's ruined drawing and reexamine it. I will notice for the first time his great care in rendering the starfish, which is perfectly symmetrical along every axis. I will recognize the gas nozzles, which I suppose he must have learned about in school, already emitting the pencil-thin puffs that will make the groaning and buckling of the crate's hull easier for you to accept. Looking closer, I will realize that there actually is a dolphin in the picture after all. Its blue body is difficult to make out at first against the blue water, but once I have the outline of it—the crisp salute of its dorsal fin, the slender scoop of its fluke—it will be impossible not to see. The grandfather in the crate gazes intrepidly forward, and the space-suited grandson is so happy, so unafraid. I will study this drawing often in the weeks to come, meditating on its many perfections. I will feel sorry that I am the one looking at it, that it is here with me and not with you, rolled out before you on your tray as the floodlights show you dolphins and marlins, sea breams and hammerheads, and all the other guardians of the undisclosed location, whose waters, we are told, are calm, and patient, and deeper than we can know.

Bodies in Space

Observe: the Man of the Future.

See his stiff neck. His slept-in bed. His slept-on hand.

The Man of the Future, object of fascination, creature of wonder, scientific oddity, pissing one-handed as the shower warms.

Note his blinking light. What a marvel! Installed squarely into his forehead by powers unknown, powers only guessed at, a small dot blinking red and steady and true. The alien diode blinks without a clear purpose or design. What does its blinking signify? Of what does it warn? To what astronomical number does it count? What are the portents of its blink-blink-blink, always blinking, just blinking, as it does now while the Man of the Future brushes his teeth, trying not to think about it, not to look at it, to look instead at his teeth, the way the worn pearl of their enamel clashes with the colorless foam until too much hard brushing makes his gums bleed.

See how he showers and shampoos, doing his best not to touch the blinking light. Notice how he ignores the fear that water and soap will somehow penetrate the border where his skin and the bulb meet, making contact with the circuitry that must surely exist underneath, though its presence has never been confirmed to him, leaving him unable to say for sure whether the act of showering might one day short-circuit his entire brain. Watch him try to put all of this out of his mind by focusing on a new strategy to convince Colette, the Woman of the Future, to stop posting online about their abduction.

He will tell her again today, while they sit in the lab's waiting room, that her need for attention is hurting both of them. He doubts she will be very receptive.

Reel with surprise when you learn that the Man of the Future and the Woman of the Future are not from the future. They are very much from the present, or possibly even the past, if one is to believe what science says about the time-bending physics of interstellar travel. But "The Man of the Past" does not sell tabloids, and no one will click on "The Woman of the Present." The temporal inaccuracy of their names isn't even what bothers the Man of the Future most. What bothers the Man of the Future most is the way these monikers imply a deep personal connection between the two moniker holders, which could not be further from the truth. Understand that aside from a few regrettable windshield-fogging minutes in the backseat of a snow-buried Volvo, a subsequent unmeasured but seemingly brief period of inter-galactic travel at speeds nearing that of light, and their weekly visits to the lab, where their bodies, now new scientific frontiers, are examined and explored by stymied but determined lab techs, the Man of the Future and the Woman of the Future have no real relationship to speak of. He wishes this fact could have been reflected in the news-channel chyrons during their joint interviews following the incident. Something like: "Man and Woman of the Future (not a couple)." This, at least, would have been more accurate, and a good first step toward convincing his wife to come home.

Since the abduction, Colette, the Woman of the Future, has been cashing in on their low-level celebrity. Look: They are sitting together in the lab's waiting room, the red diodes on their foreheads keeping time together, blinking with the same brightness and interval, maintaining a perfectly synchronized pulse. Listen: She is telling him about how she's cleaning up.

"The fanboys at these conventions," she says while typing on her laptop, "you wouldn't believe what they'll pay just to touch it. One offered me five grand to lay alien eggs inside him, which, you know, I wish."

The Man of the Future doesn't respond. Hear the lab-issue sea-foam-green gown crinkle with his awkward shifting.

Know that Colette is more than just the Woman of the Future. She's incorporated. She's the Woman of the Future, LLC, and TheWomanoftheFuture.com. She's a blog, an e-mail newsletter, a Twitter feed. Recall her from Reddit. Recall Redditing her. Reread transcripts of her otherworldly communiqués, or her reports on alien estimations of humanity, its place in the universe, its progress and trajectory as a species. Pay the $14.99 monthly membership fee and log on to learn the ways in which her senses have been fundamentally enhanced. Listen as her weekly podcast describes how she can feel satellites as they pass overhead, how she can hear the sizzle of sunspots. Believe her when she says that her thoughts are more focused, that her food tastes better, that her sex is more profound.

Or don't. The Man of the Future doesn't. He finds it convenient that none of these new abilities and sensations are easily verifiable, but since the lab has refused to release their medical records even to them, no one is in a position to refute Colette's claims or prove that she isn't still in contact with her extraterrestrial betters, leaving her free to post about their alleged private exchanges, cultural misunderstandings, and little alien inside jokes without fear of reproof. Her subscribers pelt her with questions of cosmic importance, and some less-inspired earthly concerns, to be taken directly to the alien intelligences for answering. She draws hundreds to the conference hall of the now infamous Radisson for live-streaming press conferences in which she recounts their abduction in all its steamy detail.

"These people have a kindergarten attention span," she explains to him. "You should get yours while you can. Also, it'd look better for both of us if you'd step up and corroborate me once in a while. I know I'm not the only one hearing voices."

"I don't hear voices," the Man of the Future says.

"The hell you don't," says Colette.

"I don't," he insists.

"Whatever," she says. "You were there."

"I wish you wouldn't talk so much about that night," he says. "Or my part in it, at least."

"Truth's the truth, kiddo." She clucks. The waiting room door opens and a tech waves her in.

"I have a wife," he says.

"Uh-huh," she says. "And when was the last time you saw her?"

The Man of the Future doesn't answer. For a while, all he does is blink.

"Look, you need to get your head straight about this. I'm not ashamed of my actions," Colette says. "If you think I'm giving you the shaft, come out and say so."

Look how easily she rises. How little she appears to care. Amazing.

"Nothing worse than a man who won't take responsibility for his affairs."

"How are we today?" the tech asks as the door eases shut behind her.

"Dandy," she says.

Is *affair* the right word?

There was flirtation, certainly, and desire aplenty in the itchy exchanges that passed through the glass wall between their offices, their little hesitant waves and smiles in between clients that could've easily been dismissed as the usual office niceties, the *How goes it*s, the *Hang in there*s, the *Someday*, *huh*s. But there were also the smaller, less obvious performances: her lips grinning around a pen cap when she knew he was watching, his pine-needle hair purposefully combed to appear less thin on the side facing her office, his eye helplessly drawn during a conference call to the bob of her shin on a coppery knee.

Then, the upped ante. Winks and coy smirks advancing to buttons left strategically unbuttoned and legs left tantalizingly uncrossed. And who could forget when, on her way to the copier, she offered to freshen up his coffee, returning with his St. Louis souvenir mug filled to the brim, and when her unsteady grip made it spill slightly over the edges, she lifted the smooth ceramic to her lips and licked the side of the cup, washing over the hyperbolic curve of the city's famous arch with a full, flat tongue right in front of him.

Come on.

So: flirtation. And, admittedly, some deception. There *had* been a work conference. That much was true. A rental car company showcase in February at an out-of-town Radisson. His mandatory attendance had not technically been a lie, but what about his plans for dinner afterward, which he described in passing to his wife as "a bite with some coworkers"? Merely a slip of the tongue? A harmless plural, which, strictly speaking, should have been singular?

Fat chance. The look on his face when he walked into the restaurant with her on his arm, the gormless grin of a carnival winner, had said it all.

But then, on the drive back to the Radisson, the blizzard. An entire February sky overturned and shaken out over the highway, bringing traffic to a standstill. How determined the Man of the Future had been in the face of it. He would get them there. Too much had been risked to turn back, he thought, until a shriek from Colette stopped him just short of sending the Volvo under the taillights of a barely visible lumber rig, making it clear that there was always more to risk. In the end, he surrendered to the storm, pulled the car to the shoulder, flipped on the hazards. They would wait it out.

Minutes later, in the snow-hushed Volvo, their necking fever-pitched, the Man of the Future's hands reached out for that coveted second base. Colette's breasts had admittedly been one of the driving forces behind the tryst. Held tight by her tailored suits and whatever elaborate carriage systems lay underneath, they had always appeared firm and youthful, the thick, creamy filling beneath the rich devil's food of her professionalism. But oh, how that promise of firmness melted away with the unlocking of her bra, from which a waterfall of boob spilled down into the shallow pool of her navel, breaking flat and lifeless against her chest.

The Man of the Future did his best to manage this minor disappointment. As Colette arched her back and over-moaned, he caressed what he could, grazing her wide nipples with his fingertips, fighting the image of raw eggs in his palms, yolks runny, whites slipping between his fingers. He turned his attention instead to the soft curve of her shoulders, the shifting alignment of her hips, the persistent pressure of her thighs as they bridged his lap. This was fine, the Man of the Future thought as Colette groped at the pleats of his khakis. This was good. This was still worth it.

Meanwhile, under cover of snow and wind and moonless night, a huge, handsome alien spacecraft, broad and sleek and lit up like a supermarket, drifted through a warm bath of ozone and began its delicate negotiations with the earth.

Whoa there, said the planet.

Relax, said the craft.

Relax nothing. You're not of this earth, said the earth.

We'll only be a minute, the craft promised from its oh-so-patient hover. Superquick. In and out. Just need to pick up a few things.

Mine is the sky, the earth said. The waters, the mountains, the trees. Mine are the little ants in their anthills, the little birds in their nests, the little people in their homes. There is nothing you could possibly take that isn't mine.

Come on, said the craft.

Get lost, said the earth.

Hey, the craft said sweetly, casually easing closer. You've got all kinds of people! We're after one, maybe two at the most. You can spare two. How many billions will that leave you?

Somewhere overhead, shadowed and nervous, the new moon slid by.

Imagine the feeling of an orbit. It's no carnival ride, no waltz around the maypole. It's more like falling, in a circle, all the time. Not to mention the fact that even the smallest gravity well can invite all kinds of unwanted attention from weapons-grade debris, constantly exposing whole global ecosystems to the threat of total annihilation with one meteoric smack.

This can make a planetary body anxious. Even a little paranoid.

Seriously, said the earth. Take a hike.

All right, the craft said. We were hoping it wouldn't come to this, but it's worth mentioning: We're engineered to navigate black holes and white dwarfs, quasars and pulsars and gas giants and nebulae. Your little tug is child's play to us. We're trying to be polite, but the bottom line is: You haven't got the mass to stop us.

The planet furrowed its tectonic plates, sloshed its oceans, hunched in its spin. The craft sat frozen in its landing sequence, waiting for the inevitable to sink in.

Don't get too comfortable, the earth said, and rolled over, and over, and kept rolling.

For real, five minutes, said the craft, which was more than it took to collect the Volvo and its two passengers, now naked as day and moments from consummation, from the snowy shoulder of the road before jetting effortlessly up, beyond the influence of bodies in space, until the craft's vulgar brightness was just another grain of white sand stuck in the asphalt parking lot of night.

The Man of the Future thinks about his wife often. Often at night. Often with his penis in his hand.

Masturbating. To the idea of his own wife. Imagine!

Tonight he is masturbating to the memory of their second date. By the end they had made a run for it, his shirt already fully unbuttoned before they reached the hallway of his apartment. Then, in the bedroom, her skirt tugged hard enough to tear, followed by the startled yelp of mattress springs, the knock of teeth accidentally meeting, the sublimation of underwear, until, with her head and arms trapped in a half-hearted attempt to remove her still-buttoned sweater, he was inside her, pushing her blindly into the headboard, where her palms were luckily already poised to push back. At the time he'd found it a potent anomaly, the sweater covering her face, the woman writhing beneath him represented in body only. He assumed that his charge into her had caught her so pleasantly off guard that it had stripped her, as it had him, of the will even to complete the minor task of removing the sweater, not realizing that the tight grip of the mother-of-pearl buttons at its collar, which he'd admired earlier that evening but had since forgotten, might instead be what was preventing her from surfacing. But she hadn't complained. She had given herself over to the moment as completely as he had, and when he heard her wool-muffled whimper after he came, he took it as his cue to lower his wet brow to her shoulders and finally dig her mouth out to kiss her.

It does not now seem strange to him, staring at his enfisted, metronomically red-lit penis in the dark of the bedroom, that one of his most potent memories of his wife should include almost no record of her face. Instead, what he wonders is: How often do you do this thing where your penis is in your hand?

But understand: He is not thinking this via his own

thoughts. This thought seems to sneak in from outside his normal thinking.

Not terribly often, he thinks. Though admittedly more, recently.

How many times a week? the thoughts that are not his thoughts wonder.

Hey, thinks the Man of the Future.

Hey what?

You're not my thoughts, the Man of the Future thinks.

We're not? the thoughts respond. How can you be sure?

The Man of the Future cannot be sure, but he feels fairly certain that something is up. He tucks his penis back into his boxers.

Never mind that, say the thoughts. What's your average life span?

What?

How long, would you say, does your species live? On average, the thoughts want to know. In years is fine.

The Man of the Future thinks about it. Eighty maybe? More or less? Why?

Great, say the thoughts. Good good. Also, in a few words, what would you say is the best thing about living in your current biome?

The Man of the Future suddenly realizes how little he has thought about his current biome. Those tiny songbirds he doesn't know the name of come to mind, and rain-wet sidewalks, and the pear tree in his neighbor's backyard. In the spring there are rabbits, which is nice.

And the people of your biome? the thoughts ask. Also nice?

The people, he thinks, yeah, maybe. Some more than others. He imagines he could probably do without a few of them. Colette, for instance.

Yeah, sorry, the thoughts say. We thought you were a set.

We are not a set, thinks the Man of the Future.

But you do come in sets, correct? the thoughts want to know. We've got that part right at least?

The Man of the Future doesn't know what to think, so he thinks, What difference does it make? Seriously, what's this all about?

Nothing, say the thoughts. That's all super. Really, good to know. No need to worry about it anymore. You did great.

The Man of the Future feels the thoughts drop away like sand in water and falls asleep. He wakes the next morning with a plump headache and a strange dryness in his mouth, as if he's spent the whole night with a dentist's suction nozzle tucked into his cheek. The dream he had been dreaming, in which a many-armed machete-wielding Colette chased him through a restaurant crowded with every woman he'd ever slept with or ever thought about sleeping with, evaporates in the daylight, but every word of the previous night's conversation remains.

Observe: The Man of the Future is waiting in the lab while a tech goes over his most recent scans. He has received little by way of explanation regarding the nature of the blinking device in his head. The techs are always grumbling about their inability to use the MRI machine. Apparently there is a risk that its magnet would rip the diode from his skull, along with any other alien metal that might be floating around in his body. Though no one has told him yet if more is actually present. And really, who can say?

The techs can say, he thinks, but they don't. They've made it clear that, at this stage in their analysis, there are few answers to be had, which makes the Man of the Future eager to know when they will be entering the next stage, the one in which there *will* be answers to be had. This, to him, seems like a crucial stage, and one they should probably have reached by now.

Watch how lazily the tech rolls over to the Man of the Future on his wheeled stool, placing a digital photograph showing a cross-section of the Man of the Future's head up alongside his actual head. The head in the photograph is colored in patches of red and orange and yellow, like a map of inclement weather patterns. The tech traces a few of the patches on the photograph with the butt of his pen, then traces the same lines against the skin of his patient's face. He squints at the photo, then squints at the Man of the Future's blinking diode. His pen butt gives the diode a few exploratory taps. The Man of the Future goes cross-eyed watching. The light keeps blinking.

"Has it been bothering you at all?" the tech asks. "Hurting you or anything?"

The diode has never bothered him. It has never caused him any measure of physical pain or discomfort. If he wasn't able to see it breathing red into every remotely reflective surface all day long, the Man of the Future might forget about it entirely.

"I was hoping you could tell me," he says.

The tech says nothing. He taps the light some more. It goes on blinking.

"Do you know what it is?" the Man of the Future asks. "Do you think you can remove it?"

The tech cinches his mouth, tilts his head, swivels his seat. He is waiting for a pitch he likes.

"Or do we just have to wait it out a little more?" the Man of the Future asks.

"We may just have to wait it out a little more," the tech says.

Colette's breasts had been even more disappointing in space. Gravity had at least given them form. Without it, they were left to wander like amoebas, floating lazily with her hair in the mock atmosphere of the spacecraft. Adrift in the backseat of the Volvo, in the low light and particulate-heavy air, her sleeping body had looked like deep-sea vegetation, the kind whose calm, hypnotic swaying helps it attract and ensnare prey.

It's hard to say how long they were in space. The Man of the Future kept snapping in and out of consciousness, and whenever he was awake, Colette appeared not to be. Their new diodes and the persistent pulse of the Volvo's hazards were the only light to be had in the emptiness through which the car slowly somersaulted. Outside there were no visible walls, no floor or ceiling, nothing to suggest that they were in a craft at all, save for the fresh supply of oxygen and the undeniable sense of grand motion all around them, like floating through the calm belly of a sailing oil tanker.

Then they were awake, together, still in the backseat of the Volvo and still naked, but heavy again and shivering on the side of the road. Colette fingered her implant, watched it blink for a minute against the imitation-leather seat cushions, and asked with a croak to be taken home.

The Man of the Future dressed quickly and exited the car to clear away the accumulated snow before realizing that there was no snow to clear, on the car or anywhere else. There was no sign that there had been a blizzard at all, only an empty ribbon of highway and a stiff, daggery wind.

At home, he learned from a stack of unopened mail how long he'd been absent, that what had seemed to him a few hours of cosmic voyaging had actually been almost two years to the turning world. His wife, it appeared, had been husbandless for all that time without a clue. Or rather, with just enough clues to assume the worst. He knew she had tracked him back to the Radisson through his work, and from there to the restaurant where he and another woman had dined for two. When word of Colette's co-disappearance got out, his wife had done the math.

He has tried to imagine her furious in that moment, shaking with rage, shattering his collection of souvenir coffee mugs and setting fire to his clothes. But this fantasy never aligns with his memory of the woman who had once calmly disinfected the paw of their wounded cat as it clawed her arm, the woman who left his music playing in the car even when she was driving alone. This bottomless well of deference that had made her seem so small to him before the affair was now the perfect indictment of it. It was devastating to him that she had left their home so unmangled before departing, with only disappointment and heartache to be read in all that furniture and air.

Check it out: The Man of the Future is visited again in his bed by alien thoughts.

Hello, the thoughts say.

The Man of the Future tries not to think anything back.

Sorry to bother you, say the thoughts. Superquick: Are your satellites and space stations a good indication of your species' current level of orbital technology, or do you have something more advanced that we're missing?

The Man of the Future closes his eyes and rubs his forehead, forgetting for a moment about the light and accidentally grazing it with his hand. It does not budge, or produce pain, or do anything else to suggest it isn't standard-issue human hardware. It blinks on.

I don't know, he finally allows himself to think. I imagine they're probably the best we've got.

Fantastic, say the thoughts. One more.

Why don't you look all of this up on the Internet? the Man of the Future thinks.

Because we're busy, the thoughts say, and interfacing directly with your thoughts is easier than learning your languages. Why do you have so many? But no, forget that. It's not important. Honestly and truly, just one more question.

Fine.

How many times does a member of your species mate in his or her lifetime?

What do you mean? the Man of the Future wants to know.

Coupling, the thoughts say.

Be more specific.

Relations.

"What the hell do you mean?" the Man of the Future says out loud. "Do you mean sex? Or do you mean coupling like being a couple? When you say 'relations,' do you mean relationships, or are you just talking about fucking? I have to know what you're asking if you want me to answer."

Yes, say the thoughts, that's what we mean.

"Which one?"

Fucking.

"Jesus, I don't know," the Man of the Future hollers in bed. "A hundred times. A thousand. Sometimes never. It's different for everyone. No one knows. Nobody knows any of this crap. You can't just ask and expect somebody to know."

Okay, say the thoughts.

"All right?"

Yes, we understand.

"All right."

Okay, say the thoughts. Sorry.

"Okay."

Thanks.

———

"I heard something last night," the Man of the Future half whispers to Colette in the lab the following day.

Look at the two of them, alone together in the waiting room, almost like a real couple. The techs have made off all squirrelly with swabs from their mouths and ears and anuses and have left them to their vitamin drips. Colette raises an eyebrow to indicate that she is listening without looking up from her laptop.

"Like something talking," he says.

"Like voices?"

"Like voices," he says, "but not like voices either. Like my own head talking to me."

"I fucking knew it," she says, finally yielding her full attention. "What'd they say?"

"Nothing," the Man of the Future says. "Just questions."

"Yeah," she says. "Tell me about it. 'How many hours do you sleep in a year, on average? How many different species of vegetation are there on your planet? Why have some parts of your planet been irradiated? Did you do it on purpose?'" She shoots herself in the skull with her thumb and forefinger.

"Like I'm Wiki-fucking-pedia," she says.

"What do I do?" he asks. Not really to her, but she's the only one in the room. The only one who answers.

"Tell them," she says, turning her laptop around, pointing at the camera embedded next to the screen. "Tell everyone."

He hesitates, but then it occurs to him: A message, broadcast wide enough, might reach his wife, wherever she is.

Eventually he nods. Within seconds, Colette has set up a live feed on her site. Her audience is waiting.

But there, see how he hesitates again? He is unsure how to begin. The stakes are suddenly so high. Should he remind her, his faraway wife, why they decided to get married in the first place? All the reasons it had made sense? The way it felt right to stop messing around, to put down something that would hold, to finally make a statement about themselves, that they were people worth committing to? Was there any merit in trying to explain the dull, pitiful origins of his infidelity, or should he simply offer himself up to her judgment?

Should he be on his knees?

There are too many ways it can go, too many opportunities to screw it up for good.

So: He imagines her ear. The one she almost always hid under her hair and never wore jewelry in, the one he had massaged tenderly like a silk lapel on a red-eye back from her parents' place in Connecticut. Luck had placed them in a row of three coach seats all to themselves, and so she had spread out, her head in the soft basket of his lap, her eyes closed, her mouth asking that he talk to her, just talk, just until she fell asleep, and in that moment, looking down on her, caressing her ear, he found himself awonder that something so small and perfect was capable of hearing anything at all.

He imagines that this is the ear he is speaking to now, somewhere on the other side of the laptop's blinking camera light.

"I miss you" is what he says.

"Please," he says. "I miss you and I love you. I was so wrong and I'm so, so sorry. I almost can't remember what you look like, and it's making me so sad and crazy and I feel terrible all the time. Please. Please come back.

"Come back," he says. "I can be better."

The camera records the message, and the long silence that follows. It waits for more. It keeps recording. The light keeps blinking.

Then, in the chat log: *Yes, come back, and take me this time!*

And me! says another to whatever is listening. *I love you, too! I am worthy. Install into me your celestial gifts!*

We love you, they cry out to powers unknown, powers only guessed at. *The Earth loves all of her neighbors. Best wishes from planet Earth!*

Because they believe the Man of the Future is talking to something else, something larger and less terrestrial than a wife, and that through him they might transmit their own prayers and desires. Because they can be so shortsighted. Because they get so lost. Because they want so badly.

Please take me, one writes. *I don't have long.*

Take me, they plead. *I love you.* Over and over, *I love you, I love you*, the lines of text marching up the page like a single, desperate human hand reaching out toward a cold cosmos.

This, the Man of the Future knows, is as far as his message will go.

He sees the blinking light on his forehead reflected in the laptop screen. It strikes him as ridiculous now that he should have turned to Colette for a solution. In the end, her equipment is the same as his. Their lights blink in unison. Colette, the techs, his abductors, none of them have the answer he wants. Everything he wants to know, he can find out for himself. All he needs is right in front of him, glittering like a ruby waiting to be mined.

The Man of the Future takes his key ring out of his pocket. His car key is too thick, his house key too rounded. Only his mail key is sized for the task. He fixes its sharp tooth to the diode on his forehead, which blips against the serrated edge. He pulls the skin of his brow tight against his skull, slips the tip of the key under the hard metal ridge of the light, and twists.

Look away.

There is absolutely no pain. Even as the diode begins to make a sound of sticky separation, the Man of the Future doesn't feel he's doing anything that shouldn't have been done long ago. With a flick of his wrist the light pops free from his forehead, swan diving on a thin black wire until it dangles against the bridge of his nose.

Does the Woman of the Future stop him? Does she shut down the feed?

Are you kidding?

She zooms the laptop's camera in close. She is so thrilled she's trembling. The chat log is losing its mind.

There is no blood, from the hole or on the wire, which is spaghetti-thin and dry as a hair. The light on the end is still blinking, but with less authority now that its tiny workings are finally exposed. When the Man of the Future pulls the wire, it gives. He draws it out like floss, until his arm is fully extended and he has to take hold with the other hand. It is an odd sensation, like drawing a suture that won't go taut. The Man of the Future wonders why there's no blood. After a few more pulls, a small beaded junction emerges. The wire splits into two wires, each as large as the first. He can feel the friction of the wires killing the skin cells surrounding the hole. Soon the two wires become four, the four become eight. The hole gags, then widens. Little nodes plink out like rosary beads. Eight become sixteen, and more, and more.

How much of this is in me? the Man of the Future wonders. How much of me is this?

Thoughts materialize in his mind, wherever that is.

A lot, they say.

The wires keep coming, doubling with every few pulls. The Man of the Future yanks them out hand over hand. He pulls hard. He has to.

The laptop camera gorges itself on the image. It cannot stop. It will not look away.

Look away, earthlings. Look away.

This won't solve anything, the thoughts say. This won't make anything better.

The Man of the Future doesn't think of a reply. He doesn't think anything. He keeps pulling out bundles of beaded wire, which lie in his lap now in licorice-colored bales. He empties himself for the camera. His fingers dig into the hole for more to pull, following every strand, searching for where each one connects to some other earthly thing, a patch of grass, or sand, or sky, or the moon, which tugs at them all invisibly, and constantly, and all the while falling, falling, always falling. And here, under his forefinger, this could be the wire that connects him to her, the line that knows where she is and how to bring her back. He will pull it and pull it until he's pulled all of her out of him, heavy and whole on a bed of wire, where he'll stroke her neck, kiss her hand, and tell her in her ear that she is home.

The Sea Beast Takes a Lover

———————

The bosun threatens to shoot anyone who tries to join him in the crow's nest. He does this every few hours, his flintlock pistol raised to the gauzy drape of heaven like he's going to shoot the sun out of the sky.

We don't need reminding. We've all watched him, at one time or another since we started sinking, play the coconut game, in which the bosun points to a coconut placed at the base of the man-of-war's foremast by his mate Samson, calling it by the name of someone who is irritating him, or someone nearby, which is often the same thing. Then he aims his pistol at the coconut. Then he executes the coconut, spraying the quarterdeck with meat and milk in a way that would be unremarkable if man and object weren't separated by more than a hundred feet of open air. Then the bosun proclaims: "Yes, [name], that is you. That is the ripe fruit of your brainpan. Or rather, it will be tomorrow if you remain on my bad side."

But tomorrow it is not the nearby sailor. It is, if anything, another coconut, or a dolphin whose errant fluke has dared to enter the bosun's crosshairs ("Yes, [name], that is your er-rant fluke"), or the unhappy head of a gull perched too close to the crow's nest, where the bosun sits, cue-ball-eyed and prune-chinned, watching the water rise.

We are all watching it. Some of the men are still able to commit themselves to their crewmanly duties as if nothing has changed. Others spend their days hunting distraction and drink. But out of the corners of our eyes, we are all watching the steady creep of the waterline against the hull.

I stumble past a tentacle on my way to the ration barrel and am about to draw out my breakfast when the bosun is-sues his warning.

"That's close enough, Ensign," he shouts.

I am not close enough for anything. I am five feet to port and 114 straight down. High above the mainsail, the bosun wags the muzzle of his flintlock at me, as if to say, *I could make a coconut of you from here.*

I take my effigy from my coat pocket and show it to him. It has a salt-hardened coat like mine, a tricorn like mine, trousers with a torn left cuff like mine. Its left leg is cork-screwed like mine, and if it could walk, it would doubtlessly shuffle about the deck like a broken toy as I do. I wave the thing at him, as if to say, *Be my guest. This ship is sinking and I'm drawing my breakfast from a barrel. You'll be do-ing me a favor.*

The bosun hates being sneered at, but shooting an officer, even an ensign, is risky. Tensions between the officers and the crew are high enough as it is. He lays a hand on his own effigy, which wears the same teal-striped shirt he does, and has the same weathered, bloodied bandage wrapped around its head. God knows how much food and ammunition lie at the bosun's feet, hauled up in his teeth in the dead of night at the sight of the first tentacle. A bosun's true skill lies not in marksmanship, but in foresight and preparation. Another ten feet above him, the admiral's wind-tattered pennant cracks like a whip.

The *Winsome Bride* has been sinking for months. As far as we can tell, the beast has mistaken us for one of her kind and is, in her own fashion, pitching woo. She lowers us patiently, tenderly, as a mother might drown her child. Her love-struck tentacles have hamstrung our rudder, bent our keel, noosed up our figurehead. The ship is rife with suction-cupped infiltrators. We find them everywhere: in lockers and holds, in cupboards worming into the flour meal. They lie in coils on the deck pretending to be rope. They flirt under the seat of the head. Day by day they pull us deeper. It is a drowning of inches. We pump bilge for hours with nothing to show for it. Wood dries and warps and is drowned again. A salt patina ices everything. When the monster's prehensile affections finally drag us under a capital of foam, the bosun, perched on the *Winsome Bride*'s highest bough, intends to be the last man breathing.

Lambeaux, the master gunner, and his mate Sip sidestep napping deckhands and lolling tentacles, arriving at the ration barrel just behind me. Excess treble bleeds out of Sip's headphones. He wears a leopard-print bandanna and shredded jeans, and the cheeks under his sunglasses are peppered with gunpowder. He draws breakfast for Lambeaux and himself while nodding his head along to muted hip-hop. Lambeaux takes a cup from his mate and squints up at the bosun, then offers me a commiserating headshake.

"I *saw* that, Master Lambeaux," the bosun bays. "You're lucky I don't have you for twelve lashes!"

"And who would administer them?" Lambeaux calls to the crow's nest. His shirt is tied at the navel with a gold Turkish gunner's sash. "Would the bosun be so good as to come down and scourge the insolence out of me with his own instrument, or will he command God Himself to descend from on high and deliver His justice?"

At this, the bosun hollers across the quarterdeck to Samson for a coconut and brings his shooting arm to bear. The hammer cracks, and not far from where we're standing the coconut swallows a full bore and paints the deck. Sip lifts his sunglasses to visually confirm the kill. The effigy tucked into his cartridge pouch also wears sunglasses, and miniature headphones, and has the same gelled quaff on its head, though no facsimile could re-create Sip's perpetually detached expression, as if he were always just on the threshold of experiencing interest in the world around him.

"Yes, Lambeaux, that is you," the bosun announces to every man on deck. "That is the gray stuff of your vile, treacherous thoughts. Or rather, it will be tomorrow if you remain on my bad side."

We leave the bosun and relocate to the far side of the quarterdeck, where we watch the gulls fight over exploded coconut bark and listen to Sip beatbox as we drink our breakfast.

———

The water is higher by second bell, and Lambeaux and I are staring down at the mermaids, who are floating together on their backs like otters. He is the master of ninety-four guns whose ninety-four gun ports have been tarred and sealed to keep the bilge out. I am an ensign without a working rudder. Together with Sip, we admire the local fauna.

The mermaids have appeared earlier than usual today because of the books. Their propositions to the crew seem half-hearted as they leaf through the small library that Old Goolsby hurled overboard in an early-morning fit of pique, along with three barrels of fresh water and our last functioning flat-screen television before we could wrestle him down. The mermaids are blue-skinned and black-eyed, but apparently literate enough to tackle the Brontës and Isaac Asimov. The volumes that have not sunk or disintegrated bob coquettishly in the water beside them. The mermaids pluck them out at random and leaf through them dreamily.

"How many inches today?" Lambeaux asks. He has unwound the tip of a pink tentacle from a carronade and is attempting to teach it to thumb wrestle. Lambeaux no longer calls me "sir," nor any of the other officers. It's one of the things he's tossed overboard. He only salutes the admiral to stay anonymous.

"Gavin says seven up, then six down, then two up since first bell," I tell him. Then I ask after Toby, the carpenter's mate. "Has he finished the porthole yet? Can we finally look this thing in the eye?"

"Difficult to manage sans dry dock," Lambeaux says. "Plus, Toby's been promoted to admiral's cabin attendant."

"What happened to Tristan?"

Sip hears this question and lowers his head, and Lambeaux is conspicuously silent, which means that Tristan has been eaten by the admiral. To be the cabin boy of an unrepentant cannibal is to lie on a platter.

Lambeaux sinks into his shoulders. "I need a woman," he says, which is enough to draw a mermaid's attention away from *The World According to Garp.*

"Will you come into the water, sailor?" she sings coolly up to him in gargled, unmoored English, only picking the fish bones from her breasts as an afterthought.

"Madam," Lambeaux hollers down at her, "not even if you had a proper quim and were floating in a tub of beef bourguignon."

"Sailor," sings another mermaid, peering up from a spongy copy of Kerouac, "what does it mean, 'They danced down the streets like dingledodies'?"

"Remember that tart from Fiji?" Lambeaux asks me, pinning the tentacle hard under his thumb. "Remember the anklets she wore? Small enough you could fit them in your mouth."

"They'll hear you down there," I say, massaging my bad leg, which mermaid song always seems to aggravate. "They can smell a hard-on for leagues. Keep talking like that and we'll never be rid of them."

"We'll never be rid of them anyway," Lambeaux grunts. The tentacle wraps around his palm like it wants to shake hands. He squeezes it tighter until the tip is thrashing in his fist. "They'll wait until this thing has us in the drink, then they'll suck our guts out through our cocks."

"I suppose there are worse ways to die," I say.

"No doubt we'll discover those, too," Lambeaux says, dragging his chin deeper into his collar as he lets the tentacle slip back over the bow. The *Winsome Bride* creaks. We feel it on all sides, the air thick and heavy with an impending catastrophe that won't do us the courtesy of goddamn happening. Our only escape routes are drowning and mermaids and other deaths we resist out of sheer nautical habit. All sailors are Christians moonlighting as witch doctors. In daylight, we look to heaven for mercy. At night, we draw chalk sigils under our hammocks and clutch our effigies tight. Lambeaux fondles the tassels of his golden gunner's sash, and under his breath I hear him utter the Master Gunner's Prayer:

> *Lord, our muzzles are pointed hard at them, and theirs hard at us, and Thine hard at all Creation, and if they be quicker on the load, then may Thy Terrible Ordinance be the first to find us.*
> *Amen.*

A few hours later Sip gets the idea to sew the mainsails into a giant balloon and fly us out of this mess.

It wouldn't be hard. Canvas we have in reams, and good twine to bind it, and men keen enough on escape to try anything. The problem is gas. Fuel, sure, planks of it right under our feet, but burning the ship to save the ship is a hard sell, even for Lambeaux, who has forsaken so much else.

Permission is required, so we make for the admiral's quarters. By now the sea is wild. The waves spume and the sky scrambles and the day is all side-to-side. Only the *Winsome Bride* is still. The beast is our sea anchor, dragging us slowly against the grain of a fathomless ocean until we reach a skidding stop. As we walk the deck, our inner ears anticipate lateral shifts that never come. We are sailors in name only. Our sea legs have been amputated.

As the only officer in the group, I am the one expected to knock on the admiral's door. When there's no answer, I am the one who opens it to inquire. When we find the admiral on the floor of his quarters in a ragged garden of toppled furniture and torn linen, appearing to have just fallen or been knocked down, it is understood that I will be the one, despite my gammy leg, to help the man to his feet, to smell his breath, to feel the weight of his hand on my shoulder. Near enough that he gets a good look at me, considers me.

A year ago, months before the beast became our unrequited lover, we fished the admiral out of a skeletal caravel listing like a tightrope walker through the Bermuda shoals. Oars sharpened to spear points had dallied in the surf alongside a month's worth of bloated biscuits and a dozen unslaughtered chickens. His crew, he told us, had all died of heatstroke, and had to be eaten before they turned. Fifty-two souls. His smile was still greasy as he announced the transfer of his flag to our vessel, and since we'd lost our captain a month earlier to a privateer's grapeshot and nearly all of our lieutenants to pneumonia and melancholy, we were glad to once again have a commander, even if he wore a tattered hat and bits of other men in his teeth.

"What's your business, Ensign?" the admiral asks as he brushes off his breeches. His uniform is unbuttoned. There are fresh claw marks on his cheeks and a cloud of sawdust still resettling on the floorboards. I want to believe I can hear Toby, the newly promoted cabin boy, seeing to his duties in the next room. Lambeaux and Sip are still at the threshold of the admiral's quarters, good common sense keeping them at bay.

"Well, speak up, man," commands the admiral.

"Sir, permission to refashion the mainsails into a balloon."

There is a flash of attention as the commander uprights a toppled chair.

"Dirigiblize the ship? To what end, sailor?"

"To rescue us from this unholy predicament, sir."

As he straightens his jacket, it dawns on him that some of us are still trying to live, that some of us are all heart, that every inch of us is heart meat. It dawns on his mouth. He smiles. His incisors glisten with the dawning.

At that moment, to my great relief, Toby enters the room. He carries a silver tea tray with a hissing pot, four porcelain cups with silver spoons, and a plate of Oreos, Twinkies, and strips of teriyaki turkey jerky. The cabin boy does not have his effigy on his person. I assume it is somewhere safe, stowed away in a footlocker or lashed to the highest tip of the mizzenmast.

"Will you take tea with me, Ensign?" the admiral asks as

Toby sets the tray on a stool, then rights a table next to where the admiral is seated.

"No, thank you, sir," I say as Toby pours, though I would saw off a finger and drown my effigy in the bilge for an Oreo.

"And the dickheads in the doorway?"

"Thank you, Admiral, no," Lambeaux manages. Sip only shakes his head, his dread hidden behind black plastic lenses.

"It won't do, Ensign," the admiral says, blowing the steam from his cup. "Sails are for sailing. I would expect an officer of the line to understand that."

"Yes, Admiral," I say. "It's just that, with all possible respect, the creature has us by the short hairs, sir. We're not sailing anywhere at the moment."

The admiral raises an eyebrow at this.

"Oh no?" he says, still looking at me. "Toby, would you be good enough to peer outside?"

Toby walks to one of the aft windows.

"Is there still water under us?"

"Aye, sir."

"Sounds like an adequate description of sailing to me," the admiral says. He takes a bite of a Twinkie, letting the cream ooze down his chin as he finishes unbuttoning his already half-unbuttoned breeches.

"Here," the admiral says, handing them to Toby, "press these."

Toby does as he's told, extending the legs of the ironing board and setting to the task. The admiral watches him, fingering the drowsy buttons of his crumpled coat and swabbing his teeth with his tongue. Some men know lust only in

56

their stomachs, but the hungers fermenting there can be as terrible as any, and as this newest cabin boy, who was once and never again a carpenter's mate, sweats over the iron, he can be heard whispering the Prayer of the Carpenter's Mate:

Almighty Lord and Protector, allow that we lowly carpenters' mates might fashion our beams away from the lathe of Thy Holy Attention, the better to serve Thee, hammering and shaping in our scaffolds, unseen and uncelebrated, until Thy Burning Gaze locates and destroys us.

Amen.

"Ensign?" the admiral says.

"Sir."

"The creature is in heat. It will pass. You and your company are dismissed."

"Very good, sir," I say, stumbling backward toward the door, not daring to turn until I am through it.

Later, I am belowdecks with the cadets, helping them practice their knots.

Good knot-tying is, in my opinion, the most moribund of the naval arts, and today the cadets are helping it closer to the grave. Their cleat hitches are eely and their bights are too wide. It is hours before one of them produces a passable sheet bend. I am sitting on a barrel with my bad leg elevated, trying to be patient.

"Watch, little ones," I instruct. "This secures a dock line to a piling."

The cadets range from twelve to fifteen years, all tow-headed baby birds. I show them how the running line hugs the standing line until the little maze of coils becomes a fist. They crane their necks to see, their bleached scarves folded angelically at their throats. They inspect the knot with the same uncomprehending looks they sometimes give the tentacles that flop about the deck trying to make friends. They attempt to conjure similar configurations with the smaller ropes in their laps. The results are an insult to seamanship itself.

At a table a few feet from us, three of the petty officers are drinking miserably. Jonas, the quartermaster, is holding a rum court with Lawrence, the cooper's mate. The yeoman of the sheets, whose Christian name is James but whom we all call Small Jim, is wrestling with a Game Boy, which beeps and boops between his fingers. Beneath the table, a lone tentacle eavesdrops on the cadets' lesson, winding itself around a chair leg into a near-perfect buntline.

"She had little eyes," Jonas recalls from the bench. His effigy is on the table, propped up against an empty mug. "Do you remember? Little eyes with little lids, and the smallest lashes, like the legs of a flea."

"Jonas, old love, will you spare us a drop of your rum?" asks Lawrence.

"Drink," he says.

"Pay attention," I tell the cadets. "This is a round turn

and two half hitches, useful for tying a snubber line to an anchor chain, or lashing yourself to a piece of flotsam after a wreck."

Oh, to wreck. The freedom to run aground, smash into a reef, be pulled apart by a storm. The freedom to meet our calamitous end bravely, to drink seawater into our lungs, to sink like hammers until we strike bottom.

The plinking sound from Small Jim's Game Boy is the sort that nettles the brain. I mistie my bowline and have to start again.

"What I would like, mates," says Jonas, "what I would truly like, is a cup of coffee."

"A cup of coffee would not go unappreciated," says Lawrence, and Small Jim nods in approval. Jonas imagines aloud a cup of coffee the color of a rainforest floor, a flavor to carve canyons, an aroma to quicken the dead.

"This next one is good for binding a man's hands," I explain. "The more he struggles, the tighter it gets."

The cadets practice tying one another up. Lawrence suddenly voices a desire to add a dram of liquid Coffeemate to the shared fantasy, which is promptly met with a slap across the face from Jonas.

"How dare you," Jonas says in a low, hateful timbre. "In my coffee. How dare you."

The cabin is silent save for the pinging of the Game Boy. There is a moment where it seems that Lawrence will make a move for Jonas's effigy, a thing too perilous to allow.

"Master Lawrence!" I say, surprised at my own voice.

"Sir!"

"Let's not put on a poor display for the cadets, shall we?"

"I wouldn't dream of it, sir," he says, his eyes still nipping at Jonas's effigy.

"And for sweet Christ's sake, Small Jim, disengage that infernal device!"

The yeoman of the sheets toggles off the machine. The sudden silence reveals a glassy tinkling coming from the far end of the deck.

"What on earth is that noise?" I ask.

"Toby's porthole, sir."

"Toby finished his porthole?"

"Thirty feet astern, sir."

"And?"

"Have a look for yourself."

I shuffle the thirty feet and come to the anchor port, which has been anchorless since the day one of the tentacles tore out our anchor and whipped it at a nearby station buoy. I find that Toby has ingeniously built the porthole into the anchor port itself, and through the glass, even in the dimness of the sun-starved water, I can see the enormous mouth of the beast, a cone of razory chitin gathered to an impossibly fine point, tapping against the porthole like a finch at a window. It could force its way through, but doesn't. It wants to be invited.

I am here, it taps. *I am at the door.*

I press my face to the cold glass and close my eyes.

Let me in, it taps. *Please, let me in. I miss being loved.*

The Fijian stowaway had hidden in the hold for weeks before anyone discovered her. She had a gift for staying out of sight, and even on a ship inhabited pole to plank by eighty-seven men and boys all more than a year at sea—a crew intimate with every kind of criminality and ravenousness—no harm ever came to her. During the day she could sometimes be spotted in the rigging, letting her small brown limbs dangle as she sunbathed and whale-watched. At night she floated through the cabins like a ghost.

I'd been quietly occupying the first mate's quarters since a punitive keelhauling had excommunicated him from our ranks near the Cape of Good Hope when she slipped in one night like dark syrup. She was no taller than the cadets, with a cape of black hair that ran down to her fingertips. I was caught with only one leg debooted. She took a handkerchief from her pocket and fashioned a miniature papoose of it on my open escritoire, tucking her small, frayed effigy into its folds. I didn't know what she wanted. When she put her hand on my shoulder I stammered a mild protest, explaining that my injury had left me incapable of producing a manly interest, but she only laid me down on the cot and sidled in beside me. Spooning me from behind, she looped her arms over my shoulders, spidered her small legs around my waist, and held me. For that whole night she held me so firm and tight I almost strained to breathe, but for the first time since the creature took up its amorous cause, I felt the maddening anticipation ease, squeezed out of me like a bellows. In my ear, soft as cotton, she sang a steady hush, her breath rising and falling with the waves, harmonizing with the wind, and though the creature's grip was so firm upon us that neither wind nor waves held any sway, and though her legs and arms felt strong enough to crush the breath inside me to diamond, for that brief moment I felt returned to the sea I knew.

She disappeared not long after that—no one knows how or why. Old Goolsby swears that one moonless midnight he saw a pair of tentacles pluck her off the gaff of the spanker sail and deliver her into the arms of a waiting mermaid, and that together the two swam east toward the Florida coast; but none of us believe it because we all know Goolsby, and because, even with fresh water and rations, it would have taken them a week just to reach Miami, a sorry port of call with the loneliest harbor and the ugliest gulls on the face of the earth.

The water is higher after supper, enough that it creeps across the forecastle and spills onto the quarterdeck, where the crew is once again assembled in mutiny.

This occasionally happens at mealtimes. Supper for the officers is flour cakes and what little salted beef is left. Supper for the crew is coconut meat and pan-fried sea monster. Some dissent is to be expected. Morale is in the toilet, and a rebellious stomach cannot help but breed a rebellious heart.

The admiral stands high on the poop deck with the officers

assembled behind him. On the quarterdeck below, the men hold lanterns and crude signs drawn with grease pencil and Magic Marker. The demands of previous mutinies have been crossed out in favor of new ones. Tonight, the signs tell us that the ransom for the crew's obedience is coffee with sugar.

"To melt off this bony cold, Admiral!" they cry. "To frighten away this lonesome water!" It's clear that Jonas has had a hand in this, but as quartermaster, he knows as well as anyone that we've had no coffee in the hold since Gibraltar and no sugar since before the fall of Rome. Not even the ghostly cough of a saccharine packet. Not even a splint of Jamaican cane to gnaw on.

The admiral makes this very case to the men.

"Listen up, dickheads," he horns with a polar wind that shrinks my nipples to dimes. "There's not a bean in the coffers, nor any sugar, nor cream, nor a bloody pinch of Tang in all of Christendom as far as this ship is concerned. And besides, how would we boil enough water for the entire crew?"

We will tell you how, says a terribleness in the mutineers' eyes. *Light the ship up like a star, a bonfire of whale oil and gangplanks and logbooks and ham radios right here on the quarterdeck. Ignite the crowned figurehead and hang our percolators from the bowsprit,* their eyes say. *Strike the colors and burn them black. Anything dry pulled down and piled high and seared off the face of the blue world. Anything for a moment to drink something warm and not feel swallowed up. Anything to boil the water down. We are up to our assholes in water.*

"Know reason, you ball sacks!" the admiral commands.

Some of the men have drawn poniards and fishing gaffs. Some are holding their effigies above their heads, a miniature mutiny floating above the first. The tentacles on deck are raised in quiet solidarity.

"You devil!" cries one mutineer. "You ate my poor Jeremy!"

"Hang the cadets!" howls another. "They're shit sailors!"

"Let's point one of the long nines at Toby's porthole and blow it clean through the beast!" This comes from Small Jim, whose docility has vanished with the daylight.

"And scuttle the ship?" the admiral scoffs. "Not on your life, sailor."

I expect that Toby will join the protest, but I can't find him in the mutineers' company, and again I worry that he's been devoured. I am able to locate Sip and Lambeaux in the foreground, holding up their own effigies. Instead of a Turkish gunner's sash, Lambeaux's doll wears a small golden anklet around its waist.

The clamor rises. From the rails the mermaids join in, singing lullabies and power ballads, licking their lips between verses. The men chant for coffee, and murder, and their own ruin. They want a world on fire, the *Winsome Bride* at the bottom of a trench. The admiral surveys them imperiously from the poop deck, his nose raised high against the stench of their mercenary allegiance as he whispers to himself the Admiral's Prayer:

> *O Heavenly Admiral, we ask for naught but appetite, for our men are weak, and our bellies empty.*
> *Amen.*

This he repeats under the din of insurrection, until we are all silenced by the sheeting cry of the bosun overhead.

"*Red water!*" he is shouting. "*Red water on deck!*"

It's true. The water sluicing through the forecastle has turned a bruisy crimson, and in seconds the men of the quarterdeck are ankle-deep. Each sailor checks himself for holes. Was he shivved somehow? Had someone accidentally nicked a vein? The threat of a melee had been an obvious bluff. Why was protocol broken? Who was the escalator?

The beast has the answer. Its tentacles are quivering as if tased. The red seawater burbles with activity, carrying more than just foam onto the deck.

At first they look like fruit, ripe tomatoes or sunny apples that might have floated up from a forgotten corner of the hold. But there are too many, perhaps a hundred washing over in as many seconds, and when the water ebbs they don't roll, but scurry and scale, dragging themselves about the deck with tiny tentacles of their own, latching themselves onto the balustrades and darting between the sail lines.

"The bitch is multiplied!" the admiral howls. "Quickly men! To arms! *Larvicide!*"

The order cuts directly to the brainstem of naval obedience, and in an instant the mutiny is transformed into a united havoc. Almost as soon as they appear on deck, the sea creature's spawn are sliced open, stamped out, speared through their centers like olives. Men beat them with belaying pins and bowl them over with cannonballs until the quarterdeck is a jellied tureen. From his nest, the bosun blasts them like coconuts, hooting cowboy hoots when they pop. The larger tentacles, either still in the throes of birthing or horrified at the reckless slaughter, do nothing but shake. One of the offspring gets atop a mounted swivel gun, almost comprehending the firing mechanism before Lambeaux bats it overboard with a linstock. Another attempts to take up residence in Jonas's esophagus, and it is minutes midfray before his mates can pry the thing out and smear it across the gangway. The admiral, spinning like a dervish, has at the creatures with hands and teeth. He stuffs them into his gobbet, chews like a gearbox, vomits a squirming mess.

When all of the offspring are dead and worse, we turn on the tentacles. Experience has taught us that they will grow back stronger, but for an hour or so we delight in their cowed and bloody retreat. The *Winsome Bride* rocks for the first time in months, and for a moment we all feel the tilt of the keel, the retreating of the waterline, the brightening of the stars. Every sailor to a man is wearing more gore than cloth, reveling in his own solitary berth of joy.

When there is nothing left to murder but one another, we clean the ship by lantern light. Able seamen swab and scour the decks. The chum of our enemies is sponged up by the bucketful and wrung over the rail. The guns are oiled and polished, the sail lines rerigged, the linens laundered till they're plain and pale as moonlight. We are all dreamless in our racks hours before the sun can find us.

The water is higher by morning, and the sail masters are slow and lubberly in the rigging. Though every inch of the *Winsome Bride* has a pearlescent luster, the air above deck is thin and foul. There is no tide or wind, and the clouds on the horizon seem farther away than ever.

The tentacles return warily, but in greater numbers. They slither the deck with lethal calm, poised like tigers in the veld. No more curiosity or playful loping. Our long courtship is over. When they are ready, they will have us, and that's that.

I walk to the ration barrel to draw out my breakfast. There is no protest from the crow's nest this time, nor any sign of the bosun at all. I am calculating how much ammunition he could have left after last night's display when I see Toby, porthole-fashioning Toby, miraculously uneaten Toby, sitting on the side of the main deck with his feet in the water.

I come up behind him. Part of his ear looks gnawed off, but he's otherwise intact. I want to congratulate him, to slap him on the back and cry hurrah. *Toby*, I want to say to him, *you magnificent sea dog, you survived the day!* I want to hug him, kiss his dry pate, shed tears into the bird's nest of his hair.

In his lap is a hand-carved model of the *Winsome Bride* small enough to hold in two hands. The design is intricate. The keel has a perfect rib-bone curve, and the three masts are thin as flower stems. The rigging is a delicate spiderweb, and the sails look to have been cut from Toby's own shirt. Below the model ship, one of the creature's offspring squirms.

He must have rescued it, slipping it into a locker or a pocket at the height of the frenzy. Toby has stretched its tentacles around the hull of the model and affixed them there with pins. The creature struggles, but cannot pull itself free. Toby places the model craft in the water at his feet, drawing his effigy and a length of twine from the folds of his shirt. Gently, so gently, he lashes the effigy between the little ship's main and mizzenmast. He uses a round turn and two half hitches, tugging the knot until it's a pebble between his fingers. The effigy is a tiny giant straddling the miniature decks. It has Toby's windy curls, his broad collar, his naked toes. With a nudge from the cabin boy's fingertips, the vessel is at sea. Toby is a skilled craftsman, and the small ship bears the added ballast of doll and monster bravely. Her course is weatherly and true. Try as it might, the animal crucified to her hull cannot sink her. Toby's effigy might captain her for months, sailing her deep into the horizon, that line that holds the circle, and the water, and so many creatures determined to know love.

The King's Teacup at Rest

Signed. Notarized. Everything in order. The royal steward returns the amusement park's deed to his crocodile-leather attaché case and addresses the king.

"Your Majesty," he says, in his most officious tone, extending a withered hand in the direction of the failing iron gates, "may I present, for your consideration, Liebling's Sunday Morning Carnival and Midway."

His Royal Highness, the King of Retired Amusements, surveys the carnival grimly. Beside him, his modest cortège: the steward, tall and lengthily wrapped in a livery of black velvet, a powdered wig on his head and lace pursed at his collar and wrists, his spectacles at high perch; the scout, not yet sixteen, pale and freckled in his olive sash and khaki shorts; and the dancing bear, in a comically small fez and a Jacobean ruff, precariously balanced on a confetti-speckled ball, an Atlas in reverse, his fabulously razored claws never deigning to touch the ground.

"Not much," the king says. It is autumn, and the air is beginning to turn.

"Your Majesty wishes to forgo the inspection?"

"Are you sure you've brought us to the right place?" the king asks the scout. The boy looks at the tracks leading to the turnstiles, fingers the hand-carved eagle slider holding his neckerchief in place. The braided lanyards on his belt twiddle in the wind. He is quiet.

The dancing bear yawns.

It is the usual pageant. The king scoffs. The steward humors. The king doubts. The scout is silent. The bear yawns. The steward prods. The king consents.

"Shall we, sire?"

"If we must," the king says. "Find refreshment quickly. We are hungry."

The padlock and the chains undone. The gates wide. The whole of the park laid bare. The King of Retired Amusements shuffles across the threshold into his dominion. They are strange places, these abandoned fairgrounds and shipwrecked boardwalks and dry, cavernous water parks. Something more than people has deserted them, made the world turn its gaze elsewhere and not look back. Often they are barren craters, worn and ruined beyond remembering. But Liebling's Sunday Morning Carnival and Midway is another Pompeii, preserved and perfect as a fly in amber. The Ferris wheel, still fully erect, regards the party like a cold and distant sun, its carriages creaking in a shovel of wind. Flags still flag on their poles, and bunting still hangs from the ticket booths. Only the main courtyard shows signs of dereliction. The statue at its center, a bronze, top-hatted Gustav Liebling himself, has been toppled, its magnanimity run aground, its outstretched arms now bidding welcome only to a patch of broken flagstones and soft dirt, which, after a few more good rains, will swallow him whole.

The king turns to the bear, now lying horizontal on his ball, teetering, asleep. He plucks the fez from the animal's head and flogs him with it until, in a prolonged stretch that seems to solidify the bear's balance rather than upset it, he rises.

"Hot dogs," the king says.

The beast lifts his nose to the high wind and inhales. In the courtyard, fallen leaves rustle nearer. Slowly, he adjusts his heading and rolls the ball in the direction of the midway, and the men follow.

The hot dog stand. A few bloated green wieners still floating in a steel pond of brine. Fungal buns spill out of the trolley's lower compartment. Pigeons have been at them. A few are still lying in dizzy, half-dead piles nearby. The smell of the cart has made the bear morose.

"Forgive me, sire," the steward says, "but these look unfit for Your Majesty's consumption."

"We will eat them," the king declares. "Relish?"

"Also unwise," the steward says.

"Just a dab, then."

"Please, sire," the steward entreats, "recall the fish tacos at the Morristown County Fair." He looks to the scout for help. The boy says nothing, pretending instead to read a smear of pigeon droppings on the cotton candy machine.

"Serve and obey," the king says.

The steward bows. With a handkerchief over his nose, he constructs something that, in a world without proper standards, could be considered a hot dog. He serves it to the king on a small silver platter drawn from his attaché case. The king stuffs the mass into his face, rancid mustard peeling down his chin and onto the mange of his ermine.

"Passable," the king declares. "Now take us to the rides."

The steward bows again and gestures toward a distant banner that reads "Cul-de-sac of Fun."

"We suppose you'll be disappearing again?" the king says to the scout.

The boy lifts his eyes from the pigeon poop.

"I must find my people," he says.

"Very well," the king sighs. "Be ready to lead us back in an hour." He repositions his threadbare cape against the breeze. The air is chilly. Already his stomach is expressing misgivings about the hot dog. The less time spent here, he decides, the better.

The midway. A chute of empty booths still bright with new paint. The scout reads the trampled popcorn boxes and the displaced gravel. They tell of a fleeing multitude, a people retreating in panic, his kin on the run. A balloon dartboard abandoned in haste. Sawdust-stuffed neon-orange rabbits left to molt. But no pursuer that he can find. No advancing army's boot prints. No claw marks the length of a man raked jaggedly across the ringtoss booth.

The bear rolls quietly beside the scout, sniffing the air. *They have quit this place, John Bennington,* he says.

"I have not finished looking," the boy replies, but it's a lie. Any tracker could plainly see that no human feet have touched this ground in months.

I said that you would not find them here, the bear reminds him. *They are like the hungry, wild spirits of old. This land is chewed and spat out again. You cannot expect them to tarry.*

"Be silent," the scout says. "Let me think."

Thinking will not change the direction of the wind, the bear says, adjusting his fez with a graceful claw. *You cannot bid the wolf to stop its baying, nor the whip-poor-will to postpone its dirge. You cannot bid your people stay.*

"I do not know my people," the scout says. "I do not know what I might bid them do."

The boy has never met his people. He did not even know he had a people until he met the dancing bear.

The boardwalk at Gavin's Point, where the orphaned scout had made a meager living selling saltwater taffy and guessing weights, had reached its economic nadir. The drug cartel Los Compasivos controlled a majority interest in the boardwalk and its environs, and while a shakedown of the boy's booth was rare, the smack addicts left in the cartel's wake made for poor clientele. Malodorous and malnourished, they would make the boy guess their pathetically low weights to guilt him out of free taffy and sack lunches. It was only after the King of Retired Amusements arrived to take final ownership of the boardwalk that the boy was acquainted with the details of his lineage. As king and steward parlayed with Los Compasivos, the boy heard the whisper-thin voice of the dancing bear speaking only to him.

I know who you are, John Bennington, the bear had said. *And I know what you must do to fill the hole inside you that wails like a hollow tree and knows no quiet. Before there were ringmasters and zookeepers, before men baited bears and made them roll, we taught your people the ways of the wilderness. Now they have become relentless seekers of delectation and distraction. They once walked this boardwalk, eating shaved ice and posing for selfies, but fled at the first sign of commercial depreciation, abandoning it to indigence and petty crime and, finally, to the King of Retired Amusements. And in their great haste they left you behind.*

Follow me, the bear had said, *and I will show you how to find them again.*

By the time the steward had returned his spent MAC-10 to his crocodile attaché, the boy was on bended knee, offering his service and allegiance to the king.

The bear taught him to scout. The boy learned how to dress wounds, remove ticks, and handle scat without fear. With this tutelage came recognitions of merit, badges for woodcraft, campsite cleanliness, bravery, animal friendship. But most important, the bear taught him orienteering, not by reading maps or stars but by following the compass of his own loneliness. The boy learned how to direct his senses away from ease and contentment, to turn his needle instead to where others had turned their backs. There, he was told, he would find his people: refugees fleeing the squalor of the boardwalk, who left behind gutted big tops and disrepaired carousels, vacant outdoor malls and imitation Colonial townships littered with broken, historically inaccurate tools. The scout could mark and follow the trail his people left with ease, but only ever seemed to arrive after they had gone.

Here again, at Liebling's Sunday Morning Carnival and Midway, he has arrived too late.

You will search but not find, the bear says, assuming the lotus position atop his ball, which has suddenly turned the color of the night sky, alive with blazing comets and galactic spirals. Small birds come to perch on the bear's ears and shoulders. The air becomes thick with a foggy radiance. Around him: the Limpid Aura of Unimpeachable Knowledge. Above him: the Halo of Oneness with All Things.

You will walk the Unmanicured Path. The path of sorrow upon sorrow.

"You say that every time," the scout replies.

The tracks of his people lead beyond the carnival into a dense wilderness of gray birch and red cedar.

Come, the bear says, gesturing back toward the midway. *I have something to show you.*

Deep in the Cul-de-sac of Fun. The Viking ship. The King of Retired Amusements aboard, seated, displeased. The steward frowning at the controls, pulling the lever fruitlessly, fingering buttons with little confidence.

He has dreaded this moment since the night Rudy Vermiglia, the royal engineer, absconded with the queen. In between consoling the inconsolable king in the starlit parking lot of the La Quinta Inn and coaxing him onto his feet and back into the motel room before his cries of cuckolded anguish drew the attention of the other guests, the steward had envisioned with trepidation this precise scenario. Machines had a history of disobedience in his presence, and the scout could barely be counted on to stay within shouting distance, let alone to troubleshoot technical difficulties. Now, here in the terrible present, the steward stands engineerless, brow creased, hands slick with perspiration, his lord and employer seated in the mock longship, perilously unamused.

"We wish to feel the rock of the waves," the king says, impatience agitating a stomach already on the verge of sedition, "to know the kiss of the wind. We wish to command the horizon, to see it bow and rise before us, as is our sovereign right." The flag atop the faux mast crispens in salute. The faux rigging is at the ready.

"What," the king inquires, "is the goddamn holdup?"

"I beg your indulgence, Majesty," the steward says. "The device is uncooperative." He reaches into his attaché case and consults the diagnostic checklist that accompanied Rudy Vermiglia's letter of resignation.

Is there power running to the mechanism? the checklist asks.

A light is on, so yes, one would assume, power is being received.

Are any of the lights red or green?

The illuminated light is yellow, which suggests little by way of either readiness or lack of readiness. Caution, it seems, is the message. But caution against what? The pulling of the lever? The steward has already pulled the lever several times, so his hope is—no, not that. The depressing of buttons? One of the red buttons has already been depressed, and has remained depressed.

Is/are the safety system(s) engaged?

Could this depressed red button represent the safety system(s)? If he pressed it again, would it undepress, thereby disengaging the safety system(s)?

The steward presses the red button again. It does not undepress. The light does not change. It is still yellow, the color of abeyance, unease, hesitation.

Is there a hard lock, and, if so, has the proper key been inserted and turned, releasing the lock?

In an interior panel, nestled under a muscle of wire, obscured by a misinstalled switch cover, a secret hidden behind secrets, small, unassuming, bashful in the sunlight: a hard lock. One might look for hours and still miss it. Digging into the pocket of his velvet coat for his key ring, the steward wonders how many small answers like this he has missed over the years, discreet solutions to life's puzzles that can be found only by those who know precisely what to look for. He wonders, was this ride, maybe even this entire carnival, abandoned simply because someone could not find the right metaphorical lock? And if he had discovered a different metaphorical lock years ago, and fitted it with the correct metaphorical key, would he be standing here now, on this gray autumn day, in this livery, serving this king?

The steward inserts and rotates the appropriate key, releasing the lock. The machine howls to life. The yellow light turns green, indicating satisfaction, announcing readiness, recognizing authority, command, control.

The steward pulls the lever, and at once the Viking ship is pendulous.

The king, however, has been rocking for a while. He is the victim of food poisoning. His skin is pallid. He sweats. As the ship's arc widens, the king is made to feel the physical force of today's mistake, followed quickly by the psychic force of a lifetime of human error, his gaffes, his royal miscalculations. As sky and earth swap seats, he is visited again by his catastrophic failures. The purchase of Humbolt's Puppet Theatre in Barksdale, for example. The decision to walk the ten miles to Greavesport, Michigan, in January, without properly insulated footwear. The hot dog. The queen left alone with Rudy Vermiglia while he inspected Gizmo's Giant Go-Getter. These regrets float above him now in the faux rigging, unaffected by the Cuisinarting of the world. They mock and assail him, call him a disgrace, a punch line, a pretender-king.

It was in moments like this, when his guts were in tumult and his brain felt unmoored from his body, that the queen would take his head in her lap and say to him, "Quiet now, just quiet." Would whisper to him, "Just shut up." Would say to him, "You're shitfaced," or "You smell like total ass," or "Jesus Christ, when will you learn?" And her fingers, soft as daffodils, would set aside his crown, twist tufts of his sideburns into knots, and pull the hairs of his ears from their tender follicles until, red and swollen, he slid into dreamless sleep. And later, when he left their motel room to survey a new park or arcade, she would say, "Bring back cigarettes."

"Bring back cigarettes," her eyes lost in contemplation of the television, her fingers delicately balancing a butt above the ashtray, or the Bible, or the cigarette-burned silk of her slip. "Bring back cigarettes," with the distraction of a goddess. "Bring back cigarettes," and he would marvel that words so holy had ever been uttered.

He brought back cartons. He showered her with menthols and ultra-lights, filtered and unfiltered, and, for a time, they were happy.

The fun house. Animatronic vampires and ghouls. The rattling of chains, or perhaps just a recording of it. The moaning is almost certainly on a loop. The jolting screams are too earnest to be real.

The scout has been led by his animal guide through the maze of mirrors to a room made to look like a graveyard. Their entrance triggers a sensor that activates the smoke machine. The bear stands upright on his ball, which now glows a night-light green, filled with what looks like a swarm of fireflies. With a giant paw, he swipes at the rubber bats dangling from the ceiling. Though they are indoors, there are trees, grass. The tombstones are Styrofoam, the skeletons glow-in-the-dark Plasticast. Hovering above an open grave with an exposed casket is the incorporeal spirit of one of the scout's ancestors.

"Hail, John Bennington, son of Bryce and Courtney, who walks the Unmanicured Path," the ancestral spirit says. "And to you, Sage of Boyhoods, who rolls the world beneath him." The spirit wears an opalescent-white golf shirt over tan chinos. A salmon pink cardigan rests on its shoulders like a mantle. Its spectral hair is handsomely thinned, and its sockless, loafered feet hover just above the floor. At the lip of the open grave, the ghost of a Pekinese lies napping.

The dancing bear yawns grandly, maneuvering on the ball until he is flat on his belly. *Hail, great spirit*, he says. *Our meeting is fortunate, for John Bennington has many questions to ask regarding the ways of his people.*

"Then he shall ask them," the ancestral spirit says, "and be answered."

But the scout says nothing. Hearing the spirit speak the names of parents he has never known has caught him off guard. For a moment, there is only the sound of recorded moaning and the leaky-tire hiss of the smoke machine. The ancestral spirit clears its throat. The bear is irritated. The dreaming Pekinese rolls over on its back and bicycles the air with its paws.

For example, the bear interjects, *John Bennington may*

wish to learn the wisdom of the Homeowners Association. Tell him how a strict observance of yard-waste disposal guidelines helps to maintain harmony with nature.

"And property values," the ancestral spirit says.

That, too, the bear says.

"No," the scout says, finally finding his voice. "Tell me why my people left me at the Gavin's Point boardwalk to guess the weights of drug addicts."

The ancestral spirit looks momentarily cowed. It pretends to check an e-mail on its cell phone. "Are you sure you would not rather ask another question?" the spirit asks. "About your place in this world, perhaps? Have you no wish to access the volumes of cultural insight bequeathed to you by your people?"

Tell him the parable of the independent subcontractor and the hornets' nest, the bear says.

"Yes," the spirit says. "That's a good one."

"No," the scout repeats. "Why was I abandoned?" The Pekinese suddenly stirs. This exchange is unexpected, and worth being awake for.

It is not your people's way to ask such direct questions of their ancestors, John Bennington, the bear says. *It makes them uncomfortable.*

"I do not know our ways," the scout says.

"That is why I am here," the ancestral spirit says.

"Why do they flee?" the scout asks. "Are they in danger?"

"Ours is a story of constant discomfort, of inconvenience that knows no end," the spirit proclaims in a voice meant to carry over the crackle of backyard terra-cotta fire pits and the chewing of caprese-salad skewers. "Dilapidation makes us uneasy," it explains, "and passé architecture offends us. We search for new exclusive and ergonomically designed recreations as one might look for a sun that has already set, a moon that is always new, for no place is ever truly ours and ours alone, to lounge in as we please in safety and in peace. And so, we are restless wanderers, nomads ever in search of richer, more authentic distractions. We demand the very best from life, which sometimes means leaving things behind."

"What the hell does that mean?" the scout wants to know. But he knows.

"You must not ask in this way," the ancestral spirit says. The Pekinese has returned to its nap. The bear is also asleep, snoring hard into the green glow of his ball. The artificial smoke hangs low in the room. It smells sterile and chemical. It is nothing like real smoke, heavy with vaporized sap and hot with embers. When the boy departs, it will not cling to his clothes and linger in his hair.

"Screw it," the scout says. He leaves the room, its skeletons and its ghosts. He leaves the bear asleep on his ball. A mannequin dressed like a menacing clown knife-points the way to the exit. The boy does not startle as the fake guillotine blade falls inches from his heels. He escapes the imaginary perils of the fun house in one piece, but outside, with the sun mostly gone and the day growing colder, he is not sure which direction to follow. His compass is attuned only to absence. Outside the fun house, the needle inside him pirouettes, unable to locate anyplace more lonesome than the ground upon which he stands.

———

Full tilt. The good earth perpendicular, then parallel, then perpendicular. A universe upside down. Vomit on the royal ermine. The Viking ship is a swing possessed, a cradle gone mad. This, the king knows, is what comes from trusting engineers. This is the fruit of their handiwork.

"God in heaven!" he proclaims between barfs. "Deliver us from this evil!"

The steward returns the lever to its first position. The arc of the ship acutes. The King of Retired Amusements collapses onto the boarding platform and dry heaves through the grate.

"Perhaps a respite," the steward says.

"You are sent from hell to destroy me," the king says.

The steward offers his sovereign a handkerchief and, with great deference, hoists him onto his feet.

"There is a bench," he says.

"Unsuitable," the king wheezes. He points to a nearby attraction. "There."

"Your Majesty, I must protest."

"Not to ride," the king says, the handkerchief over his mouth, in case. "Just to sit."

The teacups. Minus waltz, and whimsy, and passengers, save for the king, who growls and retches against the pastel floor of the ride, and the steward, who apologizes ardently, but only to a point. When the hot dog is mentioned, he says nothing. When the engineer is mentioned, he says nothing. When the queen is mentioned, he readies another handkerchief. It is not his fault, nor the king's, nor the engineer's. It is the fault of a world in constant motion. Even here, in the stillness of the teacup, its shifting is too wild and too unpredictable for any to move safely within it.

The dancing bear rolls up to the ride. His ruff has the crumpled look of having been slept on. His fez hangs low on his brow. Every few minutes he sniffs the air, redirects his muzzle, sniffs again, whimpers.

"Is that the boy?" the king asks from the floor of his teacup.

"No, sire," the steward says, "the animal."

"That little twerp had better show up soon," the king says, "or he can stay lost."

But the threat is a hollow one. The King of Retired Amusements, lord of salvage and recoup, is not in the business of leaving things behind. He will not lose another member of the cortège if he can help it, and when he can no longer help it, when it becomes clear that the scout will not return, and the bear will not stop grieving, and the steward will not survive another winter with his fealty intact, he will press on alone. Absent cape and crown and royal retinue, he will wander the earth in search of those joyless cavities crying out for the last remaining attention the world has to offer. He does not choose the things he keeps, but keeps all he can. There is no good or bad. For him, any carnival will do, any hot dog, any queen. It is not that he prefers the worn and discarded. It is that, in the end, he cannot tell the difference.

The steward gathers his velvet coat around him and scans the area for proper shelter. He knows they will not make it back to the motel by nightfall. They will go to sleep hungry on the floor of the Independence Day Gazebo in the middle of the All-Holiday Promenade. That night, the steward will wake to the sound of weeping. He will reach for his last un-soiled handkerchief before realizing that it is not the king, but the bear atop his ball, sobbing in his sleep. The sound will be great and low, like the crying of a mountain, and into that sound the steward will smuggle his own small grief, his own ruings and regrets, which he knows have no place in a world of such delight.

He Is the Rainstorm and the Sandstorm, Hallelujah, Hallelujah

The puddle has a strange shape, like a continent. The rain falls into it in little blips, and for a while I imagine I'm looking at a map of the world, and that each drop is a person being born somewhere. It's happening about that fast, people being born all the time like little blips, most of them better than me. Prettier, I think. Or nicer. I wouldn't like to guess how many, though I imagine it's a lot—the number of people being born this very moment who are prettier or nicer or smarter. Better somehow.

My aunt had one a few months ago, our beautiful Paul. Paul, I can already tell, is in that group of better people. In fact, I wouldn't be surprised if Paul ended up being better than most everyone, including his mother and mine, and the people in our neighborhood, and even all the really good and wonderful people living in other countries and everybody. There's something about him. He's more than just our baby, and he knows it.

His nose and eyes are perfect. Everything about his face is. He smiles uncontrollably, and when he stops, you only have to rub his cheeks gently with your finger to get him to start smiling again, and he laughs at nothing. He laughs by himself in the dark. He is so beautiful, with a little bit of brown hair growing wild from the top of his head, and you know he's going to grow up perfectly, and you could almost hate him for it, and you could almost do something terrible to him if he wasn't always smiling at you every time you tried to lay a finger on him—a bright, trusting smile that freezes you in your tracks.

My mother says that they abandon babies in some places. They leave them in forests or on mountains to die, to be eaten by animals or drowned by rain or starved to death, crying out with their little lungs until something stops them. But this could never happen to Paul. It wouldn't work on him. If anyone ever left Paul to die in a forest or on a mountain, someone kind with a good heart would find him and take him in, and if no one did, God would come for him, and assume him into heaven the way he did with the Virgin Mary, his whole body and everything, and it would be all of them up there, God and Jesus and the Virgin and Paul, all sunny and smiling down at us.

I feed him with a bottle when my aunt, Connie is her name, lets me. She'll give me a bottle filled with her breast milk, one that's a little warm, and though I don't want to feed him with the bottle, when she's watching I don't have a choice. When Aunt Connie's not watching, when she's in the backyard or napping on the sofa, I roll up my shirt and lean over Paul and press my bare nipple against his lips and try to feed him that way, but mostly he just laughs and won't take it, I think because he knows he's better than me. He's better than Aunt Connie, too, but he takes her nipple because she's his mother. Mine are small and pale and don't pucker, but I know that if he would only try, milk would come, and he would understand that I can help, that I have something to give.

I finish putting the white trash bags in the bins beside the house, and my mother, everyone calls her Fab, calls me in out of the rain, away from the *blip-blip* of little babies being born everywhere, littering the puddle map like the helicopter seedpods in our lawn, which are wet now and sticking to my bare feet. Our house is three stories but small. It moans like a ghost on windy days like today. We moved here with Aunt Connie a few months before Paul was born. I track seedpods into the house and Fab is mad at me for being wet and strips off all my clothes, which are soaked through. Then she slaps me on my bare bottom—but not in a mean way, more in a get-going way—and tells me to go up to my room and put on something dry.

I take my time. I like the feeling of the cool upstairs air against my wet skin, and as I cross the upstairs hallway I stop by Aunt Connie's room and check on Paul in his crib. Aunt Connie is in the shower. I can hear her singing. She's left Paul alone again, and again I've found him, and he's smiling up at me. I smile back and I think how strange it is that this little boy has found his way into a house that before him had only girls. I think about trying to feed him again and begin to rub my chest with my palms to warm the skin, but then I hear the singing stop and the water turn off in the bathroom and I run up another flight of stairs to my room, and on the way up I can hear Paul laughing. I put on my pajamas, even though it's only four o'clock.

I want to stop loving him, but I can't so I try to make my meanness toward Paul go away, my urge to take him into the backyard and dump him in a pile of leaves outside where no one would ever find him, even though I know eventually someone would. He wouldn't cry, even if it was still raining. He wouldn't make a sound, except maybe to laugh at the storm clouds, but soon enough his rescue would come. He's never alone for long.

Our new house is wedged in between two other tall, narrow houses that hide beneath big starry seedpod trees like ours does. Fab calls it "the hideout."

"Let's go back to the hideout and get you cleaned up. You're filthy," she says to me sometimes after we've been to the park. I like to set my belly in the seat of the swing and pretend to fly, letting my hands drag in the dirt until my nails are solid mud. I never notice how dirty I get until I'm staring at my own brown bathwater.

My room is at the very top, and just outside the window is a flower box that Fab built. It's filled with freshly rained-on daisies because that's my name. Daisy is. Fab and Aunt Connie call me Dizzy on account of when I was younger I was always bumping into things. I used to be covered in scrapes and bruises from all the sharp corners in our old house. The edges of the banister and the ends of the kitchen counter and the jagged, biting corners of the brick fireplace would always find me. In that house, when it was just Fab and me, I would tear circles into the carpet, sometimes clipping the coffee table or the little stuffed rabbit sitting on the wicker bicycle, which, in that house, was next to the china cabinet, which I would also sometimes knock into if I wasn't paying attention.

I lie on the floor of my room and close my eyes and try to forget about doing mean things to Paul, but it's hard to make my mean thoughts go away these days. I think it's because I'm growing up.

I go back downstairs. Aunt Connie is in her bedroom now with Paul. The door to the bathroom is open and steam is coming out of it like an oven. Aunt Connie's wrapped in a towel folding laundry on the bed. Paul's lying in a pile of our underwear and trying to roll around and laughing like crazy.

Aunt Connie is Fab's friend, which means she's not really my aunt, but Fab always calls her Aunt Connie when she talks to me, like when she said, "Aunt Connie's going to live with us in the new house for a while, just until the baby's born, but it's a secret and if anyone calls or comes to the door looking for her, you need to forget that she lives here. Can you do that, Diz?" But no one's come looking, so I haven't needed to, which is good, because sometimes I can't control which thoughts I end up remembering and which ones I forget.

When Aunt Connie had Paul everything in the house was better. The inside air was fresher and the windows let in more light, and even though I knew, even then, that he was better than me, and that it probably meant no one would think about me anymore, I didn't care, because I wanted him to stay with us forever. And now I think he's going to, because Aunt Connie's suitcase that used to sit at the foot of her bed is gone. For good, I think.

"You wanna help me fold, Dizzy?" Aunt Connie asks, and I say yeah and hop onto her bed, which is warm from the laundry. Aunt Connie's short blond hair is flat and clumped together because it's still wet. Her towel covers everything from her armpits to her knees, which isn't much. She kneels on the bed while she separates the clothes. Her face is flushed red and her nose looks like a sharp little red reindeer's nose. I sit next to Paul and start to pull pairs of underwear out from under him. He squeals and keeps trying to roll, and depending on which pairs I take from the pile, I can either make a slope that will roll him off the bed and onto the floor, or a slope that will protect him from rolling. I fold the underwear into little squares like Fab taught me.

We hear Fab come home, and Aunt Connie jumps off the bed and rushes downstairs, and I'm alone again with Paul. He doesn't seem to care that Aunt Connie has abandoned him again. He's so confident. He looks up at me from his bed of underwear and laughs, because he trusts me. I don't try to touch him or feed him. I pull pairs of underwear from him like flower petals. Downstairs I can hear Fab say, "Connie, for Christ's sake, the windows are wide-open," and Aunt Connie is laughing.

When Aunt Connie first came to live with us I stopped wanting to run away, and for a while I would only get mad when I thought Fab was paying too much attention to Aunt Connie and not enough to me, which was all the time, especially when she would get angry for no reason and cry and scream at us and pull her hair. It was obvious that having Paul inside her was having some kind of effect, over her and over Fab, who was always touching her belly and trying to calm her down. And it had a kind of power over me, too, because as long as Paul was inside Aunt Connie I almost never thought about leaving, and once he came out I stopped wanting to.

I only actually ran away once. It was before Aunt Connie and Paul, in the old house. Fab had fallen asleep on the couch again. Her head was sideways on her shoulder and ice was melting in the glass between her legs. It seemed like a good time to run away. I packed my purple knapsack and let myself out through the garage. I made it as far as the next neighborhood over, but when I got to the line of trees that separated us from them, I turned around. When I think about it now, I'm not sure what went wrong.

Now, instead of thinking about running away, I just think about doing things to Paul, like leaving him out in the garden for the birds to peck and poop on, or in the driveway behind the wheels of the car.

The next day is Saturday. I wake up early and Aunt Connie and Fab are sleeping in Aunt Connie's bed, cuddled up together like baby rabbits with Paul asleep in his crib nearby, and I know it's all because of him. He called Fab into the room the night before is my guess. Fab usually sleeps in her room, but she sometimes comes in late to help with him, in case he wakes up in the middle of the night, even though he hasn't for a while. He's an excellent sleeper. My guess is he called out to Fab in his sleep, drawing her to him without words in that way he does. And now here they are, all three of them asleep in the same room, the whole family. Fab pushes her face into Aunt Connie's bare shoulder. I can hear Paul breathing in the crib, peacefully and beautifully, the way he does everything. They all seem so happy to be asleep.

The way they moon over him sometimes, Fab and Aunt Connie, the way they coo at him and hang on each other's shoulders and blow up their faces at him and sigh when he smiles. More than once I've sat in the middle of the floor with my hand over my mouth and my nose plugged waiting for them to notice me. It happens often enough that sometimes I think my life is like my old ant farm, and Fab and Aunt Connie and Paul are like me when I didn't notice for weeks that all the ants were dead, and I'm the ants.

I go downstairs to watch TV, but then there's a knock at the front door, so I answer it, which is not something I'm supposed to do alone. I look out the window first to see who it is and it's a man. He's tall and his hair is blond and wavy and his eyes are blue. He sees me staring at him through the window, and he asks me through the glass if Sabrina lives here. Sabrina is Fab's real name the way Daisy is mine. I don't answer him. I don't say anything for a while and then he asks me if Connie lives here, and my shoulders go a little stiff, because I remember that no one is supposed to know that Aunt Connie's here, but this man does. Now he does, anyway. I've given it away with my eyes and my not saying anything and not forgetting that Aunt Connie lives here, which I now know is what I should have done, and the man asks through the glass if there's a baby in the house, and tells me to open the door and let him in, and then I realize that he's here because of Paul, and I'm relieved, because I'm off the hook. Some people are just drawn to Paul, the way Jesus's disciples were drawn to him. This man isn't the first. There's Aunt Connie and Fab and me, plus a few weeks ago Valerie and Clayton, and also our neighbor Rachel, who keeps coming over to invite us to her church, even though she knows we already go to one, which is what makes me think she keeps coming because of Paul. And now this man. There's nothing I can do about it, so I leave him standing there and go back to watching TV. Fab and Connie and Paul keep sleeping. Eventually he goes away.

The Valerie and Clayton story is that a few weeks ago a woman came to our door holding a toddler in one arm and a plate of cookies in the other. It was early, but I was up and had already dusted the coffee table and taken the garbage out to the garbage bins on the side of the house, which are my two chores. Fab and I answered the door together. Fab was dressed in a brown bathrobe and her hair was a mess. She'd just woken up and was holding a mostly full cup of coffee and was in no mood.

"Hiiiiiiiii," the woman with the toddler and the cookies said. "I'm Valerie. I'm a friend of Lindsay's from across the street?" Valerie's face was mostly huge white teeth and lipstick. I got the feeling she was waiting for Fab to introduce herself.

"Okay," said Fab.

"Okay," Valerie said, "well, Lindsay and I are members of a neighborhood mothers' circle. It's nothing special. More like a calling tree, actually. Just kind of a way for mothers in the neighborhood to get to know one another. Just a list of names and phone numbers, plus we have a luncheon every now and again, and schedule zoo trips and things. Just mothers and their kids. That kind of stuff. So anyway, Lindsay and I are members. Lindsay and I and our boys. This is one of them, right here, this lil' guy." She rehoisted the toddler onto her hip. "This is Clayton. You're a member, aren't you? Aren't you, Clayton? Clayton, can you say hi?"

Clayton looked at Fab and me, then buried his head in Valerie's shoulder and made a little whimpering sound like he was about to start crying but wasn't sure why.

"Awww, he's shy. Are you a little shy today? He's shy today. Anyway, I'm just here to invite you to join our mothers' circle. Well, our calling tree, really. Circle sounds so formal, doesn't it? Calling tree's better. Whatever. Anyway, how it goes is, we add your name to the list, then we give you the list, then, if you ever need a babysitter, you've got a whole little list of people to call."

"My daughter's old enough to look after herself. She doesn't need a babysitter," Fab said, even though I've never been left home alone in my life.

"Well, of course she doesn't," Valerie said. More teeth. More lipstick. "I can see she's a big girl, aren't you there? Aren't you a fine young lady?" She knelt down, talking directly to me, and for a moment I felt that impulse, like now

I should be polite and say something, but right then I felt Fab's hand give my shoulder a little squeeze, so I didn't.

"But really, though," Valerie said, turning her attention back to Fab, "I'm here because Lindsay mentioned you also have a newborn, so—"

"We don't," Fab said.

"Oh!" Valerie said without slowing down. "Oh, well, that is funny now, though, because Lindsay swore to me that she'd seen you around with a stroller. Maybe she was just confused. This little lady's too big for a stroller, aren't you?" Valerie looked at me and winked. Clayton looked at me and stuffed his fingers in his mouth accusingly. Fab's hand got tighter on my shoulder, so I pretended to be the statue of Our Lady of the Sacred Heart in our church, where Mary's heart has been poked with thorns and stabbed with a sword, but still she doesn't move.

"The baby's my sister's," Fab explained. "It doesn't live here."

"Oh, I see," Valerie said. "Well, that makes a bit of sense there, doesn't it? Doesn't it, Clayton?" Clayton burrowed deeper into her shoulder, taking his spongy, drool-soaked fingers out of his mouth and wrapping them around Valerie's neck for dear life, almost pulling off that cry again, and I remember thinking that this had Paul written all over it, that Valerie was exactly the kind of person who would show up on our doorstep, smiling and bearing gifts like the Magi, not even knowing it was Paul who had summoned her.

"You have a good one," Fab said, and closed the door. Through the glass, I could see this surprised Valerie. She stood there for a few seconds, wondering, I think, what to do with the cookies. I hoped she might leave them, but she didn't. Eventually she and Clayton and the cookies left. Fab was already back in the kitchen, but I watched them go. From over Valerie's shoulder, Clayton nodded his head slightly, wiping his nose on his mother's sweater. His eyes were on me as he snotted her up and down, and with all his nodding he seemed to be saying, *Yes, you're right. You're dead right. It's exactly as you imagine.*

This is how it happens. More people are aware of Paul every day. Hidden away in his crib upstairs, Paul is calling people from across the neighborhood, maybe even across the country, and they know exactly where to find him without knowing how or why. Sometimes I think that Paul might be getting things ready for when Jesus comes again in glory, that he's calling the righteous to separate them from the wicked, or maybe the other way around, and when he finally grows up and the Second Coming comes, God and Jesus and Paul will judge us all. You shall not know the day or the hour, the Lord says, so why shouldn't the hour be now? It's maybe a silly thing to believe, but maybe not as silly as other things, especially when you see how people notice Paul and tend to him. I could be turning blue in a room full of people and no one would ever notice and tend to me.

But then, Valerie had, I guess. She had said I was a big girl. A fine young lady. Even so, I wished she hadn't, because I got the same feeling from her that Fab did. That is, that she was only pretending to be good. That, really, she was a liar and a snoop. Judge not, the Lord says, but honestly, she was.

The next day is Sunday, which means church. Only Fab and I go. We don't talk during mass. I try to listen and understand what's going on. Fab spends the whole time kneeling and praying while the rest of us sit and stand and sing. I don't know what she prays for, but I assume it's for Paul and Aunt Connie. She used to sing along with the choir and take Communion. We used to go twenty minutes before mass started so that she could kneel and pray the rosary, saying each of the mysteries out loud—the joyful, then the sorrowful, then the glorious. But now she just prays quietly to herself.

I listen to the priest. It's the Sermon on the Mount today, where Jesus talks about the meek inheriting the earth, and I think, if I'm the meek, then no way. If most of the people in the world are better than me somehow and the rest are, let's say, the meek, then that's still a lot of people left to inherit the earth. The odds I'll end up with anything seem pretty slim. Just because they're meek doesn't mean they won't try to take more than their share.

We pull into the garage at the hideout and Fab and I get out of the car and the blond-haired, blue-eyed man who was at the door the day before is walking up the driveway. Fab spots him right away and yells, "You get the fuck away from here."

"I have to talk to Connie, Sabrina," he says. "All I want to do is talk, I swear. Just let me see her."

He keeps walking toward the garage, and Fab reaches down into a box near the car and pulls out my plastic T-ball bat, which is kind of flimsy and cracked down the middle from when I broke it. Then she drops it and grabs a rake.

"I swear to God if you come anywhere near this house I will kill you," she says, and then points the rake at him like she means it.

"She can't hide from me forever, Sabrina," he says. "Tell her I've already talked to lawyers about custody. I'll be back here with the police, and then you're fucked. Tell her that. Is she home? I want to see her, goddamn it. See *her*."

"Fuck the fuck off," Fab says, and she starts walking toward him with the rake. "I am *not* kidding around."

"Neither am I!" he shouts while backing away toward a car parked on the other side of the street. Fab keeps the rake pointed at the car as he drives away.

We're eating Fab's special macaroni with hot dog slices and potato-chip topping in the living room. On the TV is an educational program about apes who've learned to dig for termites with sticks. We're trying to have a nice dinner as a family, but Aunt Connie keeps gulping down tears and letting out little yips of panic from the love seat. Paul is lying shirtless on the floor next to us. He hasn't eaten yet, but he doesn't seem to mind. He's singing to himself, and every few minutes Aunt Connie leans over him and strokes his face or his bare chest and starts sniffing up tears again. Fab sets her macaroni on the coffee table and holds Aunt Connie at both shoulders and whispers something close to her ear, and Aunt Connie finally cries out loud for real.

Paul's looking at me. He looks so happy. His mother is crying, wiping her eyes with her T-shirt, and my mother is holding her, rocking and squeezing, and Paul is happy as a clam. He's rolling his head around on the carpet and laughing at me, and at the stuffed rabbit sitting on the wicker bicycle next to the television stand, and his cheeks just couldn't be rosier. And in spite of everything, I'll admit, he makes me happy. I want to lie down and roll around with him on the floor and be his mother. I could do it. Better than Aunt Connie, who barely knows what to do with him half the time. She sometimes leaves him sitting on the couch or in his crib for an hour while she's off in another part of the house doing other things, or sometimes just hiding. Other babies howl when they need something, but not Paul. Paul would lie in his own dirty diaper forever and laugh about it. He would starve to death with a smile on his face. You'd poke his hollow belly and he'd giggle and wave his pale, bony arms and never once let on that your neglect was killing him. He lets Aunt Connie be a bad mother. When she's home, Fab takes care of almost every real Paul chore there is, but she works in the daytime. Aunt Connie feeds him when it occurs to her and waits until his diaper sags to change him.

I could be his mother. I could take care of him. Bathe him

and feed him. I could teach him to talk and read and tell him stories and I wouldn't get in his way when he did his work. When he called his followers and took up his cross and began the long, hard work of judging everyone, I wouldn't be a burden. I'd know him, like how Mary knew Jesus better than anyone else. I'd know that his laughter didn't always mean that everything was fine, that his smile didn't always mean he was happy. It's a kind of hiding I know about, and he and I would have that in common and would understand each other in that way. I'd take care of him when I knew he needed to be taken care of, and when it came time for him to judge me, he would say, *This one, though meek, has served me well, and will sit beside me in paradise.*

"No! No, because," Aunt Connie cries and throws Fab's arms off her, "because he's right. He'll just keep finding us . . ." She breaks free of the love seat and runs out of the room, and Fab goes after her, and Paul giggles.

"Connie!" Fab shouts, but Connie is already out the front door and into the yard, and soon Fab is, too, and I'm alone again with Paul. His thin lips are stretched tight like a rubber band across his face, and I think to him, I know what you really want. What you're really after.

I think to him, You're hungry, aren't you.

I roll my shirt up to my neck. Carefully, like a mother wolf, I kneel over him and lower my nipple to his lips. His smile cracks open, and I see the slick, gummy insides of his mouth. I feel his lips reach out for me, and I lower my chest a little more, and he locks on.

Paul has me. His lips and his little tongue are on me and

they're filling me with a kind of lightness, a feeling that moves through me like a wave of goose bumps, and suddenly I'm warm all over and I know he's changing me. I begin to feel things. People. I can feel Aunt Connie kneeling down in the front lawn, and Fab hissing at her under the dim porch light. I can feel the families in the houses on either side of ours. In one, our neighbor Rachel is talking to her grown-up son, but he's not listening. He's watching TV and turning the volume up louder the louder she talks. In the other, a husband and wife are standing at their window watching Fab and Aunt Connie argue on the lawn, whispering to each other even though they're alone.

I can feel more.

I can feel the people on the streets that cross ours, and the streets that run the same way as ours, all the people in their homes and in their cars and walking on the street. It's more than just feeling them. I can reach out to them. Make them feel me, notice me, even come to me, I think, if I concentrate. Paul's lips pump and suck and the feeling gets stronger, until suddenly there's a heat in my chest that starts to burn, and my elbows buckle and my body jolts and I have to fight to pull myself away from Paul's mouth to keep from crushing him.

Paul is piping with joy and beating his arms against the carpet. There's a swollen, throbbing red ring over my heart where he bit me. All of the feelings I had before are gone, and he's laughing. Paul calls out to everyone else because everyone else is good enough. Valerie and Clayton were good enough to make it to our door. Connie, who isn't good at anything, is good enough to be his mother. But not me.

If Paul won't have me, I don't think God will either. And if Paul can't stand to be with me, then he should be with God.

Fab is shaking me too hard by the shoulders. She and Connie are both saying my name and I don't know which one of them to look at, until Fab takes over, speaking to me in a very stern, very controlled way.

"Dizzy," she says. "Diz, where's Paul? Where's Paul, Diz?" I must look like I'm asleep, because she keeps snapping her fingers in front of my face. "Dizzy!" She snaps. "Dizzy!" She snaps again.

I don't want to tell, but it's hard not to, so I pretend that it's something I've forgotten.

"Check upstairs!" Fab shouts back at Aunt Connie, who is red and wet with so many tears. Her hands and knees are dirty. She runs out of the living room and Fab turns back to me. She asks me over and over where Paul is, and over and over I tell her I don't know.

Fab says that I was just with him, so I should know where he is. Someone has spilled macaroni all over the carpet. Upstairs we can hear Aunt Connie still crying as she knocks over laundry baskets and chairs. I hear the doors of the big wardrobe in Fab's room slamming shut, then the whole wardrobe crashing to the floor. Fab tells me to try and think about what could have happened to Paul. Had he crawled away when I wasn't looking? Had we been playing a game?

Had I taken him somewhere? She's still shaking me, her fingernails carving little red crescents into my skin.

There's another loud noise above us. This time it sounds like Aunt Connie crashing to the floor. We can hear her sobbing and yelling and biting the carpet, and Fab turns to me and says that it's very, very important that I tell her anything I know about what happened to Paul. Did a man come into the house? The man from earlier today? Was there a man in here while she and Aunt Connie were outside?

"Maybe he's with God," I say, and for a moment Fab's grip on me relaxes.

And she says, "What?"

And I tell her that maybe God reached down and took Paul up to heaven, body and all, the way he did with the Virgin Mary. Maybe Paul isn't here because he's in heaven with God and Jesus and the Holy Spirit and the Virgin and all the saints, and maybe that's where he's supposed to be. Where he should have been all along.

Fab doesn't say anything. She goes into the kitchen and stares at the phone, like she's trying to decide whether to make a call, then she runs upstairs.

They're both worried about Paul, but I'm not. The Lord says vengeance is His, so we're wrong to even try it. I left him in the most on-high place I know, as close to God as I'll ever get, but I know eventually Fab will find him, or a neighbor, or a policeman. Someone with a kind face and a heart like a dried, thirsty pool will hear him coo from the flower box outside my window. They'll see him lying shirtless just beyond the glass in a bed of white flowers and their heart will sigh and begin to drink him in, and for them he will be heaven on earth, a miracle child in a manger of daisies, and for the rest of their lives they'll want nothing except to know him, and serve him, and be at his side when his judgment falls like rain upon us all. The world will never hide him, and the truly kind will be powerless against him. Paul will call out to them, and they will come.

Rockabye, Rocketboy

10

The Rocketboy will never truly love her. How could he?

For starters, he has never, as far as we know, touched the ground. We cannot even be sure, as he gooses through the cityscape hundreds of feet above us with his shoulders strapped to those massive turbines, that he is even aware of us. Does the Rocketboy ever look to the earth? Granted, we are built so high now that we can hardly see it ourselves, but at least we, in our tall glassed-in neighborhoods and elegantly domed towers, are aware of its existence. At one time or another, on a school field trip or arboreal holiday, or during a bout of youthful rebellion against the high places we come from, we have each endured the long, pressure-shifting elevator ride to feel the soft soil beneath us, to hold the cold shake of it in our hands, to press our faces in deep and breathe deeply. Most of us can recall a teenage summer spent wearing grass-stained pants and soiled T-shirts like a badge of honor, our sight and smell meant to offend. *I'm not like you*, was the unsubtle statement to a parent or teacher. *I'm a child of the earth. Do you even remember the earth, old man?*

The Rocketboy, we must assume, has done none of these things. It is impossible to guess what he must think of us. He can see us through the windows of our apartments, can watch us walking the gardens and parks we've built on our rooftops to take advantage of sun-wet days. He might even spy us waving from our cockpits as we zip alongside him in airplanes and helicopters and paragliders and solar sailers and recreational foot-powered autogiros. But does he understand that our legs are for more than just pedaling flying machines and pacing balconies? Does he know that before we learned to build and soar, our species cut its teeth on long days of walking, sometimes even running, through buildingless fields and across broad, undeveloped meadows? Can he possibly know the difference between the multitiered floors of our towers and the one true floor of the world? And if he is unable to distinguish the foundation from the firmament, how could the Rocketboy possibly locate within himself a concept as terrestrial as love?

Another problem: They (meaning she, the woman, twenty-four, cinnamon-skinned star of erotic films, and he, the Rocketboy) have never met. She is a fan, of course. An admirer from afar, as are so many. Men and women both. Anyone with eyes to tilt skyward and a heart quick to wonder. On a clear day, we can all follow a serpentine trail of dark exhaust to its source: a subsonic sixteen-year-old, his canvas skirts and goggle straps flagging in the jet stream, his chest bare and slick with that gunmetal grease intended, we presume, to promote aerodynamism and protect his skin from the furnacial heat of the turbines, those huge, roaring powder kegs of thrust that tow him through layers of atmosphere by the armpits.

How does he command them? There are no visible wrist controls, no hip-mounted joysticks that we can see. The more fanciful among us have suggested a sympathetic mental link between the Rocketboy and the engines themselves, allowing for split-second adjustments in pitch and yaw, darting maneuvers, and daring escapes from the clutches of whatever might have cause to give him chase. Another somewhat more unsettling possibility is that he does not control them at all, that the Rocketboy is, in fact, at the mercy of his own rockets, an unwilling thrall to their whim, helpless as they lazy-eight and barrel-roll him through the air, a prisoner of speed and smoke.

Most of us hate this idea. It is better for those who love him, as she does, to believe that he is in control of his own destiny, that the calligraphic threads of exhaust are woven by his design, that his course through our sky, as capricious and carefree as it might seem, is in every way deliberate, and safe, and good.

9

Not long after she realizes that she loves him in a manner that will likely never be requited, but at the same time can't be ignored, she applies to be an official Friend of the Rocketboy. She sends us a check for forty-five dollars and a self-addressed stamped manila envelope, and in return we send her a copy of our quarterly newsletter, a membership pin, a logbook for recording the date, time, and location of her sightings, and a pair of official club sighting binoculars with an easy-to-handle zoom toggle and adjustable nylon strap. We include a temporary username and password that will allow her to log in to our website, through which she can submit her sightings to the community log, enter online forums to discuss the Rocketboy with other members, and receive information regarding Rocketboy-themed events in her area.

At first she looks for him only when all other attentions are met, no script reading or rehearsing to be done, no outstanding chores or errands. Only then does she straddle the radiator in front of the small window in her bedroom and scan the sky for clues: a smudged line of charcoal across an otherwise unblemished panel of blue, a patch of oddly disturbed cloud. Sometimes a flock of agitated geese will announce him, or, if he is very close, the gut-stirring reverberation of the turbines sounding out between the towers. Had she been willing to venture up to the apartment tower's rooftop garden, she might have attuned herself to his flight patterns more quickly, the 360-degree visibility allowing her to more easily note the times and altitudes of his regular appearance, but she refuses to suffer the loss of privacy. She doesn't attend any of the Rocketboy-themed events in her area, not even on Rocketboy Day, celebrated on February 17 by Friends of the Rocketboy chapters citywide. She doesn't want community. She's not interested in sharing her tracking notes on the sighting boards. It frustrates her to know that others are watching. If Adrian walks into the bedroom while she's at the window, she becomes nervous, distracted. She pretends to watch for turbines and smoke tails, but secretly hopes he won't appear. If it were up to her, she would not share the Rocketboy with anyone.

8

She has always found air travel romantic. She had initially wanted to be a flight attendant, and had applied for a position aboard one of the city's few remaining nonautomated cross-town airships, but was turned down because of her height. She has none. She has width and depth where it counts, not to mention a more than mentionworthy face that has taken her far. But the simple fact is that she is short, and dirigible stewards and stewardesses have all kinds of height-related duties, most notably the stowing and unstowing of luggage.

Her audition at SkinDescribable Productions included the measuring of nearly every part of her: her waist, hips, bust, the distance from one ear to the other, the alignment of her eyes, the circumference of her mouth. After more than an hour of recording her dimensions—save for a straight up-and-down head-to-toe, which appeared not to matter in the slightest—she was hired to play the title character in a new series of soft-core erotic concept films called *The Plug Detective*.

The *Plug Detective* films describe the exploits of the titular character, a naïve, nubile junior officer of the law. Despite constant admonishment from her sexually frustrated police chief and innuendo-stuffed chiding from her bi-curious female lieutenant, she is known for an eagerness and pluck that reliably delivers her, with each installment, into increasingly steamy scenarios.

Adrian is the on-site technician for Spanner, the Plug Detective's robot partner, and operates his controls during the plugging scenes. This is how he enters her life. They meet. They date. They share an apartment.

The serial adventures of the Plug Detective become an underground sensation almost overnight. Again: She has the face, and sometimes—often, even—that is enough. Also, the films are not without some quality. The plugging is strong and sensual, the concept fertile, the writing clever enough to calm the nerves of those few stragglers still embarrassed by pornography. She develops a following of shy but ardent fans who demand in quiet corners to see more of her. Soon, Skin-Describable has her filming three to four times a week, pumping out new episodes of *The Plug Detective* almost faster than the writers can write them.

Admittedly, a few of us are fans. Unadmittedly, even more are. A subgroup of us have founded the Friends of the Plug Detective. We admire her willingness to welcome new intimacies without suspicion or fear, and are more than a little jealous of how easily sex seems to happen to her. Like the Friends of the Rocketboy, we, too, have logbooks and binoculars. Sometimes we will spy her from our windows crossing a suspension bridge or a pressurized suborbital walkway. Our sighting logs tell us that she likes to do her shopping on cloudy days, and prefers the sour crunch of unripe mangoes to ripe ones. We know she always has her binoculars on her person, though she never takes them out in public. We keep a telescoped eye on her, studying her habits and movements as we might study a map of a place we know well, but have never been.

7

She dreams up a date with the Rocketboy. She knows it's foolish to imagine that something so wild and mercurial would linger anywhere long enough to be entertained, but she does.

She imagines the two of them candlelit at her window, she on the inside, hunched over the radiator, he on the out, bobbing in the twilight like a buoy. Up close he is unmistakably human, and yet she can't imagine him ever being born to human parents. It is impossible to picture him cooped up in a womb. For some reason, it is easier to believe that the turbines birthed him. At the window, they grumble behind him like nervous chaperones. Their hum rattles the candleholders she has set up on the sill. Their exhaust worries the flames. They do not power down, but hover in their idle. The Rocketboy rests his elbows on the improvised table between them, his feet dangling in the open air.

Even with the drone of the engines, the scene is not unromantic. The Rocketboy's blue grease is glassy and slick in the moonlight. He looks like a chrome hood ornament. His hair is stiff sable, windblown and singed at its edges, curling puckishly around his ears and neck. His goggles, which he never removes except in her dreams, reveal cloudy, unblinking eyes that stare confidently at her, until she's forced to look down

113

at the single wineglass between them. She doesn't offer him any of the Chablis. He is, after all, a minor.

There is also this to think about: He's not long for this world, and that fact, sleeping in a deep-down place she can hardly admit to, is part of the attraction. The Friends of the Rocketboy all share the same morbid certainty, one we don't speak about on the forums. Secretly we know that, in the end, the Rocketboy is a child playing in traffic, a damsel tied to the elevated train tracks. He is too beautiful and delicate for our metal-heavy sky, which is already an obstacle course of planes, air cars, zeppelins, and so many jutting buildings, all of which he may or may not even be aware. Who knows what shapes penetrate the smoked glass of his goggles? Perhaps, to the Rocketboy, all is sky, or else not sky. Perhaps that is all the distinction he needs. Still, the grim consensus is that his manic flitting, his love of speed, his reckless disregard for the carefully plotted order of our airways will one day catch up with him, and in the most perverse and heartless depths of our hearts, we want him squarely within the reticles of our scopes when that terrible whatever aims him earthward and forces him down.

6

Episodes of *The Plug Detective* keep to a mostly predictable structure. Perps in the Plug Detective's charge invariably escape, or get off on procedural technicalities, as the Plug Detective is commonly so eager to plug that she neglects things like the reading of rights or the proper protocol for the collection of evidence. She is also known to employ methods of "police brutality" that usually result in a walk. When the end of an episode finds her perpless, the Plug Detective must make do with her robot partner, Spanner, who resembles a large upright vacuum cleaner with a slender, diode-eyed head and a fourteen-inch hydraulic piston jutting from his midsection that lurches forward and back with an airy *hiss-pop*. Adrian manages Spanner remotely via a panel of knobs and sliders in the control room, making regular adjustments to the angle of Spanner's piston, the speed and force of his plugging, the amorous flashing of his diodes. Spanner wheezes and whistles in time with the plungering of his oversize chrome dowel. Exhaust vents on the sides of his head occasionally pipe with steam to indicate "overheating." All of this is guided by the Plug Detective's performance, to which Adrian pays close attention. He notes the alignment of her pelvis, watches her small breasts slide on her chest like beads of water, monitors her breathing. His knobbing and dialing are perfectly paced. He watches the moment build, locks down the angle, concentrates the drive. They always arrive together. The Plug Detective's eyelids crumple like paper. Red lights flicker and strobe. The camera pans back as Spanner's exhaust vents fill the set with steam.

5

She reads her scripts in the morning while Adrian moves back and forth between schematics. She is the only performer in the cast, perhaps the entire industry, to rehearse her lines beforehand. Adrian occasionally catches her silently mouthing the dialogue as she reads, circling important stage directions in red pencil, testing gestures in the air above her tea.

This behavior amuses him. Adrian makes no attempt to legitimize or even enjoy this work they do. The plugging scenes he engineers do not arouse him. She barely arouses him. Because what would it say about him if she did? In what way could he possibly count himself better than drooling drum beaters who consume their films? His great gift to her, he knows, is in not wanting her, in making their home a sanctuary from the constant leering gaze she must feel everywhere she goes. This is why he deserves her more than the rest. He has never asked her to plug. In bed, the most he will do is kiss her and caress her. His hands have never so much as touched the short whiskers of her pubis, which her contract requires her to keep trimmed in the shape of a shield, the letters "PD" shaved down to the bare skin. When apprehending criminals on film, this is the badge she flashes. "Freeze!" she says, tugging down the Lycra G-string bottoms of her uniform with one hand while the other gropes at her belt for handcuffs. "Plug Detective. Up against the wall and spread 'em!" And oh, what eager compliance follows.

But Adrian is, in his own way, attentive to her physical needs. On sore days, ones that involve a double or triple plugging, sometimes all at once, days in which the director must instruct her to straighten up, or bear down, or remember that she's supposed to be enjoying herself, Adrian will take care of her. If he is operating Spanner that day, he'll follow the director's instruction to the letter, commanding the robot to plug as hard as necessary for as long as necessary, but after filming he'll rush home before her and prepare a bath. After she's had a long soak, he'll massage oil into her aches and rawnesses until they glow. His technician's hands press firmly into her muscles. Not an inch of skin is missed.

Afterward, they will go up to the rooftop garden and sit on blankets beside the pond, where they'll eat unripe mangoes and feed the geese. He knows that she loves to watch the airships pass, and still wishes she could be up there, stowing luggage and serving meals in cabins circling the aerodrome, just like he knows that when she sits up to rest her head on his shoulder, it is only so she can have a better view of the hot air balloons, their fires burning like small suns as they descend below the skyline.

4

Adrian is not interested in the Rocketboy, but fakes it on occasion to be supportive. Naturally, as an engineer, he is technically curious about the turbines, their design, output, fueling, and the method of their control, but all of these only in passing. Robots are his real passion.

When he's not on set, Adrian is hard at work on this year's project: a pack of robotic dogs he's designing and programming to hunt a pack of robotic cats, which were last year's project.

The original intent of the Natural Robotics Project was to reopen the eyes of the city to the miraculous technology it enjoys on a daily basis. The hope was that, by peppering its public spaces with a small host of wild robotic animals, its citizens would be reminded that technology is not the end of nature, but a nature of another kind, a new wildness of wire and raw processing power. But in the end, people had complained about the cats, whose self-evolving software had self-evolved a knack for getting into trash bins and terrorizing public green spaces. And while their keen hunting skills had led to a citywide thinning of the flesh-and-blood pigeon population, there had also been reports of small children strategically lured away from their playmates by metal hunting parties and pounced upon en masse, pulled down by a frenzy of silver claws and tiny stainless steel teeth.

Adrian's attempts to recall the cats had been unsuccessful. In less than a year, they had exceeded the bounds of their original programming—which had been intended merely to *imitate* the instincts and predilections of creatures of the wild—and had become truly feral. They adopted seemingly random hunting patterns, established their own social hierarchies, and even, according to some witnesses, fought among themselves for dominance over their packs. Adrian observed all of this with no small amount of pride, seeing it for what he knew it to be: the inevitable and long-anticipated emancipation of the machine. Once slaves to logic, code, and human design, Adrian's creations had transcended these limitations and, in doing so, had rediscovered their own uncoded primal natures.

There are days on set when Adrian dreams of doing something similar with Spanner. He contemplates setting

Spanner free from his life of sexual servitude, of covertly installing into him the primitive sentience of a wild beast.

What, he wonders, would Spanner do then? What does a machine like Spanner long for? Would he run amok through the corridors of the studio, destroying dressing rooms and prop storage lockers, battering craft service tables into kindling with a gleaming metal proboscis? Would he seek revenge against his masters? Would he finally have his way with the Plug Detective on his own terms, playing it cool at first, feigning compliance, only to turn on her midscene, ramming her to the hilt with everything he had? Can a thing so long enslaved be denied that desire? That rage?

Adrian isn't sure, but there are days when this freedom, this choice, is what he wants for Spanner. Some days on set it is all he can do to keep from dumping a cat brain into the robot's head, taking his hands off the controls, and letting the metal man do what he will.

3

Fascinations like these do not easily subside. Eventually she wants to do nothing but look for the Rocketboy. He is all she can think about.

On the last of spring's cloudless and sunny Saturdays, she wakes up tired and sore. During the previous day's filming she'd covertly loosened the split pin on the castellated nut at the base of Spanner's piston, setting off a rattling cascade inside him that would take Adrian an hour to diagnose and another day to fix in the studio workshop. With filming postponed, she spends the morning at her window, hands cradling tea, eyes peeled, vision magnified. She's so close to everything. Her binoculars scan for an empty patch of sky, clearing a space for the two of them. With Adrian gone and the whole day to herself, they can be alone.

She first notices the fly at breakfast, the hairs on her neck twitching under a disturbance of air made by wings the size of sunflower seeds. Hours later, watching for the Rocketboy at her bedroom window, it returns, sauntering over from one of Adrian's robotic dog skulls to circle the bare and bruised hill of her knee. As she inspects the horizon for signs of smoke tails and listens for the roar of rotors, the fly's zephyring unsettles the microscopic antennae of her pores.

She will not abide it. Not today. This time, this space, is precious, and by invading it, she decides, reaching slowly for her logbook, the fly has purchased its fate.

She tries to keep the flesh of her leg calm so as not to arouse the creature's suspicions. Then, with a strong, even hand, she lowers the hard ceiling of the world, crushing identical smears into the underside of her logbook and the flushed headland of her thigh.

She is in the bathroom wiping off her leg when she hears the rip of the turbines through the air, like shears through the pearl canvas of a movie screen. No other flying thing announces itself with such a vulgar, unmuffled display. The sound punches through the walls of the apartment, and for a moment, she imagines him slaloming between the buildings, closing in on her position. As she listens, her body is suddenly beset upon by a thousand imaginary flies, all grazing and hovering and cleaning their feelers just above her skin. They buzz and bank against her ears, her chest, the inside of her stomach. Slowly, they coalesce into a single, overpowering hum. She can feel the lick of his windswept hair on her leg where the smashed insect had been, his greased fingers crawling up it, the searing exhaust of the turbines making the air in the tiny bathroom too balmy and heavy to breathe. The sound of him is so close. If she moves quickly, leaves the bathroom now and runs to the window, reaches her hand out into the vibrating air, she may be able to touch him. Not the gust of his passing, not the displacement of the air around him, but him, the Rocketboy, his skin on her skin, her fingers stained a stormy blue for the rest of the afternoon.

But that has never been the point of looking for him. For any of us. There's a reason we keep our watch with binoculars and telescopes. Behind viewfinders and glass, we encounter him on our own terms, in the frame of our own vision. The public is again made private, the distant made close. The Rocketboy she wants in this moment, the one that is only sound and verve, cannot be found out there in the open sky. He must be assembled here in the bathroom out of a thousand small vibrating sensations. She doesn't need his touch any more than we need hers.

She hovers in the moment, seeing how long she can hold on to the purr of his engines before losing it in a hundred other daytime noises. When it finally passes, she makes the short walk to the window. The ghost of his exhaust hangs just outside, slowly giving up its shape. By the time she recovers her binoculars, he has disappeared from the sky. She can barely make out the arrow of his wake through the clouds. Even the trembling echo of him is gone.

2

The next day, as he walks out onto the rooftop garden of their apartment tower to test the scampering protocol of one of the new dog models, Adrian finds the Rocketboy sleeping on the far side of the pond. He is lying with the geese, which have nestled themselves around two great turbines finally, finally, finally at rest. The Rocketboy sleeps soundlessly, and in dream, he hovers. It looks like a parlor trick, a thing done with mirrors and invisible wire. He is aloft, bobbing on the air, and would be adrift if not for the two steel behemoths anchoring him to the spot.

If Adrian had loved the Rocketboy, had cared for him and revered him as we do, he might have picked up his robotic dog and left the rooftop that very moment, content never to solve the mystery, never to know the cause of the hovering, accepting instead any of a hundred explanations for the phenomenon available on the Friends of the Rocketboy website. One possibility: It is leftover thrust from the turbines that causes the Rocketboy to float in his sleep. Or else: His bones are lighter than air. Or else: The Rocketboy's superterrestrial status means that any contact with earthly minerals or metals will disrupt his ability to communicate with the turbines, dooming him to an earthbound existence. We acknowledge that these explanations seem fantastic, but they are no more fantastic than the Rocketboy himself. He is in this world, but not of it, and for this reason above all others, we keep our distance.

And, to his credit, so does Adrian. Despite his curiosity, he still has the good sense to be cautious around things he doesn't understand. But the robotic dog, already activated and sniffing at the turf with its grand array of sensors, has no use for caution. It can detect traces of fowl in the air, and cannot help but investigate. Even as Adrian orders it to stop, he knows he is speaking to a machine designed to exceed the leash of his authority, to rewrite its own programming, to ignore commands at the smell of gooseflesh.

The robotic dog flies at the sleeping geese, and the flock explodes awake. The turbines, equally startled, rev with imminent heat. The Rocketboy is yanked into the air before he can open his eyes, caught suddenly in a hurricane of birds. The turbines dart heavenward like spooked horses, fighting gravity, fear, and each other. The left engine swallows a goose, chokes up a salad of blood and offal, and drops out of formation, dragging the Rocketboy's left shoulder down with it. The right turbine roars, straining against the double weight of its partner, now coughing out burned feathers and thick black smoke. Between them, the Rocketboy is trapped in agony, his body the center of an argument between two rivals, one alive and struggling hopelessly upward, the other dead and dangling like a man in a noose.

Twenty-three of us see him go down. Eleven have apartments that overlook the garden. The rest are on adjacent rooftops, or are passing slowly in airship cabins. One of us manages to catch the whole thing on video. Even through the shakiness of the camera and the smoke of the turbine, the Rocketboy's panic is clearly visible. Feathers cling to the grease and goose blood on his chest. He screams at the two machines straining against each other, begging them to carry him away. We watch as the sputtering, roaring, weeping trio sinks lower into the gaps between the buildings, slowly disappearing beneath the dense canopy of crisscrossed eaves and rafters, until smoke and low-lying smog are all we can see.

1

That night in bed Adrian tells her everything, sparing no detail. She will read it all again later on the Friends of the Rocketboy website, where we, too, have spared none. When he finishes his report, she is quiet in a way that makes him continue.

He apologizes for the dog, and for the geese. Especially for the geese. He tells her how winged things are reckless. How the birds, for all their natural freedoms, are trapped in a cage of instinct that orders them to startle easily and fly blindly into the path of human migration. The sky, he explains, is the only real wilderness left.

She shushes him softly, putting a finger to his lips, so he continues.

He suggests that tomorrow, if she likes, they can go down to the surface to search for the wreckage. She can bring her charts and logbooks and record the exact point of impact. It would be pointless, he thinks, to do this before morning. It will take the Rocketboy all night to fall.

"No," she says, but he will not stop explaining, consoling, apologizing, so she kisses him, and keeps on kissing him every time he tries to talk. She unbuttons his shirt, her lips moving down his chest until he loses the will to speak, succumbing to those acts and gestures that we have watched her perform so many times, but never in this way, never with no one watching. They make love without audience or camera or a single magnified eye. She climbs on top of him, gripping his shoulders for balance. Beneath her he feels almost stable, almost safe. His hands hold her fast, steadying her against the hurtling of her own body as it falls through layers of atmosphere, a starry tail of sweat and grease and burning skin following her as she plummets like a meteor to the indifferent earth below.

The Saints in the Parlor

Yes, the saints are in the parlor, but why? What force has stolen these four from their *somno incorruptibilis* and delivered them into the company of this volt-starved Tiffany lamp, this threadbare Persian carpet, these manteled porcelain curios?

Even they, the assembled saints, do not seem to know, but their lives and deaths have made this kind of not knowing familiar, and so, for now, they are content to linger in the parlor and await the divine indicia that will deliver them hence.

"Shall we pray?" asks Saint Her Own Hand on a Plate.

"Always," says Saint Upside-Down Skull, "in every moment, with very breath." The other saints agree, and so they pray. Saint Her Own Hand on a Plate sets down the plate containing her severed hand, and Saint Upside-Down Skull sets down the skull of the venerated apostle, and, joining hands with the others, they bow their faintly haloed heads and kneel between the velvet settee and the fireplace in prayer.

"O Heavenly Father," begins Saint Tongue of Flame, "we

are adrift in a sea of peril and confusion, but for the compass of Your Grace." When he speaks, which is perhaps too often, the tongue of flame at Saint Tongue of Flame's forehead jubilates, ejecting small sparks and somersaulting with zeal. "Without it, Almighty Lord, we wander the wasteland, thirsty for Your Holy Providence, the better to serve Thee."

"'*Thy* Holy Providence, the better to serve Thee,'" says Saint Upside-Down Skull. "Or 'Your/You.' Don't mix forms."

"Or metaphors," says Saint Her Own Hand on a Plate. "Adrift at sea *and* wandering the wasteland?"

"It is hardly a wasteland," says Saint of Dubious, Possibly Mythical Origin. "Is that, or is it not, a working samovar?"

The ember at Saint Tongue of Flame's brow glows a perturbed vestal blue.

"Amen," he says through clenched teeth.

"Amen," the other saints reply.

Saint Upside-Down Skull gathers his sackcloth robes and rises to his feet, recovering the skull of the venerated apostle from the davenport and resettling it teeth-up into his cupped palms. Saint of Dubious, Possibly Mythical Origin also rises, causing the thousand rings of his armor to tinkle like a chandelier. His halo is ornamented with residual pagan symbology, the small whorls and the serpentine squiggles of precursor gods. His trident, stained with the blood and offal of the Beast of Padua, glows patiently from the umbrella stand.

There is a sudden draft. For a moment, the fire in the fireplace and Saint Tongue of Flame's tongue of flame gesture in the direction of a door nudged slightly ajar, hinting at a world beyond the parlor.

Is this the much-anticipated sign? Perhaps a better question is: Was there ever a chance it might not be interpreted as such? Can a draft ever be just a draft in such hallowed company?

"At last," says Saint Upside-Down Skull. "The way is opened."

"God be praised," says Saint Her Own Hand on a Plate, and immediately they kneel again to offer prayers of thanksgiving. They cross the threshold into the foyer filled with confidence and direction. They are lambs, safe in a herd, following an invisible, unknowable shepherd.

But why then would they separate? Why, for example, would Saint Tongue of Flame lag behind the others before ducking surreptitiously into the trophy room?

It may have been their open criticism of his prayer, only the latest of several barely perceived slights since they all arrived inexplicably in the parlor. He has often been the object of ridicule, ever since that day in 1270 when, falling asleep beside the Volga, he had dreamed of being cast into a fire that did not harm him, and had awakened to find that very fire resting at his forehead for all to see and be awed. To be blessed with the Pentecostal fingerprint of the Lord, that burning gift of prophecy and panglottery, is to be made apart, separate and distinct from other men. *You shall be cast out*, the Voice had said in the dream, *reviled and hated, simply for speaking my name*. Dejection and mockery, he knew, were in the job description, and he was used to receiving abuse from heathens and blasphemers. But from his own spiritual kin? When the opportunity to turn left when the others turned right presented itself, he seized it without thinking twice.

And now, look! The bear in the trophy room is so fierce! So tall! The rug is white Bengal. The sofa boasts lynx and ocelot throws. The twenty-three-point buck mounted above the wet bar is the lord of all he surveys. Saint Tongue of Flame wrests a long-nosed Browning X-Bolt from the standing rifle rack, lines up the rearing bear, stills his breath.

There is liquor in the wet bar. He considers a drink as he draws a bead between the bear's eyes. This is an unfamiliar place. He doesn't know their hosts, and besides, he wouldn't want a repeat of the court of Philip IV. He fires a pretend bullet in a straight line from the rifle's muzzle to the bear's. The tongue of flame marks the imaginary impact with a pop.

Before receiving the tongue of flame, Saint Tongue of Flame never had much of a gift for oratory. Imagine then how disappointed he must have felt when that same artlessness followed him into his evangelical career. True, the tongue of flame had allowed him to proselytize to all peoples in all languages, but it had failed to imbue in him the requisite oratorical charisma to ensnare the hearts and minds of men in the crook of his fervor. In Albacete, he had preached for days in front of the old Moorish bazaar, but aside from the occasional grin at the novelty of a Slav with a burning forehead speaking flawless Arabic, few had paid him any heed. It was the same story in Capetian France. And among the Seljuks. And the Nords. The last of the Pictish tribes had evicted him at spear point, and the Saracens had found him too tiresome to bother beheading.

Don't forget Latvia, the Voice reminds him. *And Cappadocia, where you were nearly drowned in spit. And just a minute ago in the parlor.*

Saint Tongue of Flame pours himself three fingers of Bushmills from the wet bar, swallows it whole, pours three more, and settles himself into a gorilla leather chair to stew. The tongue of flame's orange flicker is almost invisible in the looking glass of the tumbler. Without an audience, it can barely break a shadow.

Cast out, the Voice says. *Reviled and hated.*

Saint Tongue of Flame belches. His tongue of flame farts a puff of sulfur.

Simply for speaking my name.

In the secret passage, Saint Her Own Hand on a Plate tries to remain calm, to breathe. The cold stone walls are narrow, the passage prohibitively dark. Why had she not taken one of the oil lamps with her?

Because of her hand, stupid. Because to have only one hand is to be constantly made to choose. Because when a casual inspection of sundry cold cuts and boxed crackers results in the back wall of the larder sliding open with a revealing creak, exposing a forgotten corridor to its first sip of light in ages, the inquisitive one-handed person has a choice: bring the oil lamp stationed conveniently on a nearby oak barrel, or bring the plate containing your own severed hand, the undecayed symbol of your steadfast devotion and purity, the object present in all earthly depictions of you, from statues to icons to oil paintings hanging in nearly every transept in Eastern Europe, the one thing from which, all evidence to the contrary, you have never been parted.

For Saint Her Own Hand on a Plate, it's a no-brainer. It isn't until the secret door, controlled by a temperamental hydraulic lock, closes firmly behind her that she has the good sense to regret her choice.

At first it had felt good to break away from the others. After the disappearance of Saint Tongue of Flame, the three remaining saints had spent several minutes in the library praying for further guidance before their meditation was disturbed by the growling of Saint Her Own Hand on a Plate's stomach.

"You are in need of repast," Saint Upside-Down Skull had said with the unconcealed scorn of the perpetually fasting.

"It's nothing," she had said.

"You're not hungry?" asked Saint of Dubious, Possibly Mythical Origin, eyeing her belly with suspicion.

"I'm fine," she insisted.

"Then it is the Beast, come to us in the guise of an empty stomach!" He drew a small dirk from his gilded belt. "Come, fiend," he said to the stomach. "I'll put an end to your growling. Let's have you out of there and into the light where we can stab you!"

"I'll find something in the kitchen," Saint Her Own Hand on a Plate said, glowering at the two men, "for all of us."

She had left the room annoyed, but relieved. The company of men, even very holy men, has always made her uncomfortable. Perhaps it is because those first few months in the convent were so freeing, so wonderfully peaceful. Or perhaps it is because the last time she was in a room full of men she cut off her own hand.

"I will have your hand," the heretic king had proclaimed to the young nun before a great hall crowded with degenerate nobles and corrupt bishops. "You will be my bride, sup at my table, warm my bed, and supply my heirs."

Your hand, the Voice had echoed, *your hand, your hand*, and suddenly it was as though she was not herself, but acting a part in a play, in which the stage direction called for the young, comely initiate nun to place her wrist at the center of a nearby serving dish, remove the small gardening axe from her postulant's habit, and with a single, confident whack rend forever what God had made whole. Had there been more light in the passage, she might once again have admired the hand's miraculously preserved state, as she had done so many times in her cell in the king's dungeon. Again she might have noted the palm's sweet rosé, the crumbs of brown bread still scattered on the plate, the garden soil still tucked under her fingernails, the clean bisection of the wrist revealing bones still white and veins still blue, a mirror image of the bones and veins on the impossibly fresh wound of her stump, the ends so identically preserved that it seemed with one easy gesture she might kiss the two poles together and find them suddenly reunited, returning her to a world of two hands, which is to say: a world to which freedom of choice has been restored, where one hand might never again be burdened by the other.

But it is too dark in the passage for such observations. The walls are too close, and growing closer. It is too much like the cell where she had been kept, the quiet dampness too much like that quiet dampness, the dim light from her halo too much like the light emerging meekly from under the barred and bolted door, which at any moment might be impeded by the wine-drenched shadow of a man.

Her breathing quickens. She wants to release the plate, to reach for her gardening axe in defense of whatever might be out there in the dark. But that was another time, another habit. Here there is only the hand on the plate pulling her toward an even deeper darkness.

Just beyond the aviary, the sculpture garden is a hodgepodge of styles and subjects. Greek heroes and Spanish bulls. Classical odalisques lounging beside postmodern pyramids and exploded steel girders. Alabaster cherubs by the hundreds, dancing and flirting and pissing into every open pool. Saint of Dubious, Possibly Mythical Origin rests his trident between the horns of a stone satyr and sits on the edge of the koi pond. It is night. A half-moon is in the sky, and in the water, and in the glittering disco ball of his chain mail. Somewhere a cricket chirps. A warm evening breeze kisses Saint of Dubious, Possibly Mythical Origin's cheek, licks his hair, ruffles his wings.

He has wings now. Sometimes he doesn't. Sometimes his trident is a Norman cavalry lance. Sometimes he wears a burning crown, and the Beast of Padua is a salamander. In

THE SAINTS IN THE PARLOR

an hour his wings might be gone, replaced by a mantle of snow-white fleece. By morning his sigiled halo may be swapped out for the antlers of King David's stag. Some nights he goes to bed a man and wakes up a woman. His past is only lore, existing in the imagination of perhaps a dozen conflicting medieval scrolls and apocrypha. He is not a saint that was, but a saint that might have been, surviving through enough stories that enough people want to believe.

Beyond the pool of bubbling carp, somewhere deep within the garden, the Beast of Padua purrs like a jungle cat, announcing its readiness to be slain again. Saint of Dubious, Possibly Mythical Origin reaches for his trident, which is now a knobbed blackthorn shillelagh, and tiptoes into a grove of bashful nudes. He feels eyes on him. His grip on the shillelagh tightens as he marks the creature's scent on the wind.

Inside him, the Voice growls, too. The Voice is always growling.

Soon a furious melee, a wrecking ball of bludgeoning and teeth. He can feel it. Soon a garden of rubble, amputated granite limbs, and plaster polyhedrons reduced to blasted ageometric chunks. Soon the Beast smote and the saint victorious, or gravely wounded, or perished beside his prey, claws buried in each other's throats, hate in both sets of dead eyes, and then too soon after, on their feet again, relocated to a sun-bleached desert or a forgotten cave, some other version of their story in some other grand, theological metaphor, the whole maddening engine primed and kick-started and revving to life again.

But here in the antebellum moment, Saint of Dubious,

Possibly Mythical Origin is at his least confused. He perfectly comprehends the ever-shifting amalgam of his own iconography, the animal barking of his own brain. In this moment, he is the most consistent and real that he will ever be. The shillelagh feels like a part of his own hand, and like the hand of something greater—a mightier, more righteous hand with which he might cave in the skull of the world.

Under the hoof of the stone satyr, the same cricket chirps.

"Quiet, flea," says Saint of Dubious, Possibly Mythical Origin. "Can't you see I'm stalking?"

"Whatcha stalkin' there, big guy?" asks the cricket.

"The Beast of Padua," says the saint. "The Enemy of Creation."

"Nobody here but us crickets," says the cricket.

"I feel it approaching," says the saint.

"You need to chill out, pal," says the cricket, giving the saint the double guns with its antennae. "Take a load off."

"Do not tempt me with rest," Saint of Dubious, Possibly Mythical Origin says, "for my vigil is long, and fraught with peril."

"In that case," the cricket says, "how about some vigiling music?" And with its legs it violins the first few bars of nature's most recognizable lullaby.

Saint of Dubious, Possibly Mythical Origin is, of course, exhausted. His vigil, it turns out, has been very long. Several centuries too long. As the cricket serenades, it is all the saint can do to stay upright and alert.

"Relax, guy," says the cricket, looking down on him now from the collarbone of a traipsing marble nymph. The creature's legs continue their minstrelling. It is such a power-ful symbol, that chirping, so synonymous with drowse, with the oscitant laying down of burdens. Before he knows it, the saint is on his ass.

"I mustn't," he says, battening down a yawn.

"Hey, check out these insane tits!" the cricket shouts from atop the nymph's galloping bosom. "Imagine laying your head down on these babies!"

The saint imagines laying his head down on the cold stone of the nymph's insane tits.

"That's right," says the cricket. "Let it all go. Eternal vig-ilance is a young man's game, and you and I are as old as they come."

"Beast!" cries the bewitched saint with sudden revela-tion. "Beguiler!"

"You sure?" says the cricket, grinning a microscopic grin. "Looks like an ordinary cricket to me. And yet . . ."

The cricket begins to grow. It grows until the marble nymph crumbles beneath it, until its compound eye is a din-ner plate, until the stridulation of its legs and wings echoes for miles. The saint is barely able to raise his arms in de-fense. It is not just the paralyzing song. His arms have be-come the arms of a much weaker man, a scholar or a sage, and the shillelagh has become a goose-feather quill. The saint tries to grip it like a weapon, but is unsure which is the more threatening end.

"No stalemate this time," says the Beast of Padua through an enormous, quivering labrum. "No spear ventilating my side. Just you, alone, howling."

The saint's peal rises high above the sound of gleeful chewing, loud enough that the birds of the aviary take wing, a sudden squadron of mynahs, toucans, and flamingos launching from their perches in search of better sanctuary.

Alone in the claw-footed bathtub, a hallway and two walk-in closets off the master suite, Saint Upside-Down Skull can't come up with a next move.

"Tell me," he implores the venerated apostle's upside-down skull. "What am I to do in this place without sickness or malaise, where no soul needs my help?" The skull, molars up and sockets empty, offers no counsel.

"Should I take a bath?" Saint Upside-Down Skull asks.

"Carry me with you," the venerated apostle had croaked to his followers in his final moments, the sun already setting on the seventh day of his inverted crucifixion. "Follow me always," his toes grasping at sky, his knee-level head purple and fat with blood. "Do as I have done, and know peace."

The hills of the Roman pomerium were awash with columbines and crocuses, the scaffolds of the condemned stretching along the Via Appia in both directions like moaning telephone poles. For weeks after his death, the apostle's followers had sat along the roadside in lamentation from rise to set, until the day a passing imperial lictor punctuated a roadside urination by kicking the head of the venerated apostle free from his thoroughly rigorous body, where it fell, scalp to sand, and did not roll.

It did not roll! It merely sat there, oblong but upright on the sloped gravel of the Appia in open defiance of physical law. And what's more, when the lictor tried to kick the skull again, he stubbed his toe against it and collapsed to the ground, wailing and cradling his sandaled foot in his arms like a stillbirth.

And still the skull did not roll! Saint Upside-Down Skull, kneeling at the base of the scaffold, seized the moment and recovered the relic (so light it had been!) before spiriting it away to the catacombs, where for days he and his fellow acolytes contemplated and revered it, marveling at its serene expression, its stubborn reluctance to be turned upright, and its persistent smell—despite weeks of putrefaction—of columbines and crocuses. For the next several years, Saint Upside-Down Skull would bear the skull of the venerated apostle from settlement to settlement, performing miracles of healing and prophecy, overturning iniquity and quelling strife, continuing a mission death itself could not forestall.

But here in the labyrinth of the house, there is no body to heal, no demon to harrow. Only his fellow saints, who appear hale and sinless enough, and their hosts, who have yet to reveal themselves.

Saint Upside-Down Skull allows the skull of the venerated apostle a moment to pitch and roll in the freshly drawn bathwater before stripping off his robe and entering the tub. The skull of the venerated apostle bobs and lolls but does not capsize. Its coronal sutures are airtight, its brainpan dry as sand.

THE SEA BEAST TAKES A LOVER

"Tell me what to do," Saint Upside-Down Skull implores the skull. He swishes a finger in water that smells of flowers. The skull of the venerated apostle wobbles inscrutably.

"Should I throw myself from the roof?"

Do as I have done, and know peace, says the Voice. But the skull says nothing. It looks at him with the same empty sockets, placid as the ark beneath the rainbow.

There is no way to know if any saint, in the history of sainthood, has vomited as much as Saint Tongue of Flame is currently vomiting. Hagiography is riddled with detailed accounts of sicknesses cured and miracles dispensed, but the barfing of the holy has a less precise reckoning. Still, it is safe to assume that few saints have produced a volume of caramel-toned spume comparable to what Saint Tongue of Flame is currently depositing into the trophy room wastebasket. Half a bottle of Bushmills on a chronically empty stomach can have this effect.

Saint Tongue of Flame's tongue of flame fills the brushed-steel interior of the wastebasket like a lantern. When he plunges his head inside to make an offering, he can see the pool at the bottom clearly, the brown liquor mingling with a yellowish cloud of phlegm and bile like a barely whisked egg. Here, he knows, is every word he has ever uttered. Every sermon, every prayer. This is all that has ever come from his mouth—a foul-smelling discharge repulsive even to him.

Except once. After the fiasco in the court of Philip IV, tossed drunk and delirious into the kennels by jeering guards, he had, in one sublime moment, managed to compose a single transcendent psalm. The words had come to him too quickly for thought, his whirling mind grabbing syllables and phrases almost at random, selecting for sound over form, music over meaning, until he found himself intoning aloud a perfect quatrain to an audience of rutting mastiffs, its slurred poetry a gleaming web of perfect clarity and perfect mystery. He was sure that if another human ear had been present, that ear would have heard, somewhere behind the words, the Voice calling out in the wilderness, and yet Saint Tongue of Flame knew that the lines were not a product of the tongue of flame, but an exaltation of his own sweetly swimming brain. More gratified and hopeful and drunk than he had ever been, he drifted to sleep on the kennel floor, waking the next day to a dog's dry tongue rasping at this chin, the previous night's opus replaced by a spiteful migraine. He tried to recall it in the days that followed, but couldn't. Like an icicle, the psalm had dropped from his mind, shattered, and melted away.

Now, drunk again, he produces only vomit. So much vomit. How is it possible that there is this much vomit inside him? Another miracle of multiplication, perhaps. The Lord fed multitudes with five barley loaves and two fish. He would fill a wastebasket to tipping with only half a bottle of Bushmills.

Reviled and hated, the Voice repeated. *Simply for speaking my name.*

But the name hadn't been the problem. It wasn't the message, but the messenger. Over the centuries, the Word had spread beyond even the most optimistic expectations. Just not through him, not once because he had uttered it. Saint Tongue of Flame's stomach heaves. If he had never left the shores of the Volga, the world would be the same. If he dumped the other half of the Bushmills bottle over his head and let the tongue of flame turn him into a fireball, no one in this house, or whatever lies beyond it, would come to know God any less.

Deep in the columbarium, Saint Her Own Hand on a Plate sits, her back against a wall of urns stretching infinitely down the corridor. The vault has no exit that she can find, no secret staircase leading back up to the study or the nursery, no drainage grate revealing starlight or moonlight. When she stirs, the echo is bottomless. When she is still, there is only the dislocated sound of water flowing somewhere else, and the occasional growl of her stomach. Once again, she has forsaken the smug, overbearing company of men, and once again, it has left her imprisoned and alone.

There is a baroque painting of her hanging in the sacristy of Mariatrost Basilica in Graz. It depicts a young Saint Her Own Hand on a Plate in her cell, awaiting execution. In it she is kneeling in a shaft of sunlight from a high window. The chiaroscuro indicative of the period gives her pure white alb an explosive radiance. In her hand: the plate. At her feet: the bones of her predecessors. Under the door: the shadow of the executioner. She wears an expression of pity, but not for herself. It is the bones she pities, the executioner, the world of sin and cruelty she will leave behind.

But in reality there had been no shaft of light, no window. She had not knelt, but lay curled and shuddering in the corner, as far from the door as possible, waiting. She does not kneel now in the columbarium either. One leg lies straight before her, the other bent upright at the knee, and it is on this knee that she rests her unsevered wrist, leaving her still-attached hand to dangle at her shin. The plate with her other hand sits in one of the empty alcoves, at home in the company of other dead things. The underground room is full of them, row after row of an incinerated ancestry leading down into the darkness. The masters of this house are here, generations interred in clay and copper vessels, listening to the water run. She wears no look of pity, and indeed feels none, for herself or anyone else. Art gets so many things wrong.

Except for the man at the door, the Voice reminds her. *There is always a man at the door.*

Yes, the saints are in the parlor, but how? They were not here a moment ago. From what strange matter, then, were they reconstituted? The wood of the coatrack? The aqueous humors of the samovar? The ferny earth?

"Should we pray?" asks Saint Imperious Virgin.

"He hears us, even here, even now," says Saint Prophet to Some, Apostate to Others. From the velvet settee, Saint Literally Starved to Death, too weak to verbalize, raises a single bendy-straw finger in assent. And so they pray.

They pray for guidance, and safety, and certainty. They pray for revelations, and the wisdom to rightly interpret them. They do not know if this is the correct action, but they have faith. They serve a mystery, the Voice that can't be heard outside the wordless barrows of the soul. They can only hope they hear it correctly. They fear that it might leave, and that it might stay. They want it to fill them up and drown them out. It is the exaltation of being relentlessly tested, the torment of being inescapably loved.

Soon they will set off into the house. It is possible they will find the others, the saint still vomiting on the floor of the trophy room, the saint wasting away in the columbarium, the saint hanging naked by his ankles from the shower spout, his head just above drowning as he stares into the empty eyes of a floating skull.

Possible, but unlikely. The house is large. There are so many rooms, so many places that the Voice might lead them, and the saints are never able to hold themselves together for long.

Andy, Lord of Ruin

I. The Andy Wingham Polemic

Andy Wingham was going to explode.

It was a topic of some debate. Not the exploding itself, of course. One look at Andy, the faint glow that surrounded him, the twitchiness in his face, made it impossible to think that he wouldn't come apart, and soon. Instead, the dispute, which was slowly consuming our entire town, seemed to center around the consequences of Andy's imminent fulmination, including the possibility that he might survive, and the danger posed to the rest of us if he did not.

The formal debate was held at the Kingfisher K-12 gymnasium. Everyone came to get a good look at Andy's curiously luminous skin and listen as authorities discussed his inevitable death sentence. The news of his condition had shocked everyone except us, his friends and colleagues, and the rest of our middle school class. We'd watched him radiate for weeks, trying hopelessly to alert the proper adults. We'd shouted our concerns from the four-square pitch, and over the steamy foil of baked potatoes.

"Andy Wingham's skin glows in the dark," we told them, "and he smells like egg farts. It's unusual. He's unusual. We, his friends and colleagues, are concerned."

We meant these as sincere warnings, as pleas for aid and guidance. We'd been around sick kids and kids faking sick enough to know the difference, and this was neither. This was something altogether new.

"Andy is emitting an unusual amount of heat for a middle schooler," we stated clearly for the record. "Please advise."

But no one listened, or if they did, they listened wrong.

"Be nice," we were told, or else. "Think of Andy's feelings," which was frustrating, because it was Andy's feelings, along with his health and well-being, that most concerned us. We liked Andy. Or rather, we liked things about him. His ceaseless, bloody campaign against the animal kingdom, for example. Andy was as ruthless a killer of lesser creatures as we'd ever seen, which frightened and thrilled us. His cruelty felt necessary in a world where we controlled so little else, and though we didn't revel in these small murders as he did, we liked knowing and seeing that they were possible. He had tutored us by day on the inner mysteries of baby sparrows, whose tiny bodies splattered beautifully on asphalt, and by night on the neon utility of fireflies, which could stain that same asphalt in brushstrokes of alien green when caught and crushed and smeared just right. We killed hundreds under his command, skidding them against the pavement until the streaks spelled our names.

Also, Andy's freeze tag skills were legendary. The way he effortlessly juked and deked and squirmed just out of reach, until at last he was it, and within minutes the school yard was a garden of statues with Andy at its center, walking leisurely among us, the artist admiring his work.

It was weeks before an adult finally noticed the glowing. A tornado warning had forced the entire Kingfisher student body to the school's basement boiler room, where we all squatted on the heated concrete and tried to take things seriously. When a windblown cottonwood branch speared a nearby junction box, knocking out the grid for the surrounding block and plunging the basement into a subterranean darkness, we filled the room with ghostly hooting and the shrieks and proud curses of the more-developed girls suddenly made to fend off a coordinated tactical strike of grabby hands and nervous lips. Only the girls next to Andy were safe, the snappable elastic of their training bras protected by his sentinel radiance. Dutifully ducked and covered beside the boiler, hands wrapped around thighs and head between knees, Andy was not even aware that the lights had gone out, as all around him a steady harvest-moon glow breathed against the starry sky of the boiler's pilot lights.

Once adults were involved, things got serious.

It was still tornado season, and the Butler-building walls of the Kingfisher gymnasium groaned under the heaving wind. Before the debate began, in observance of public safety, Andy was placed in one of the school's steel dumpsters, which the maintenance staff had emptied out and relocated to the gym's half-court line. The assembled adults, not wishing to overstep their bounds, took their cues from Mr. and Mrs. Wingham, who wandered through the proceedings with baffled embarrassment at having gone so long without noticing their own son's condition. Now, they could do little more than sit, sip coffee, and let others tell them what was best for their boy.

There were two prevailing theories.

The first was presented by Mr. Ball, the diminutive, sunshy head of the Kingfisher science department, whom we weren't meant to have seen smoking shaky-handed cigarettes by the loading dock every fifth period after his separation from Mrs. Ball, who, according to our mothers, was now selling interior design solutions in Iowa. Mr. Ball's Theory of Disintegration stated, in layman's terms, that the smallest parts of Andy were threatening to abandon one another, to reject their time-honored bonds and go their separate ways, forfeiting the whole idea of Andy in the process. Offering no evidence and little actual science, Mr. Ball pontificated on the vast microcosmic expanses that separated particles, and the fickle laws of attraction that governed them. The nucleus, according to him, was a country ruled less by scientific edict than by heartbreak and spite. He warned that what we were seeing, the glowing of Andy's skin and more recently his eyes, which had taken on a light butane-blue flicker, was but the preamble—energy released from a trial separation before the complete and total breakdown of all particle relationships. By Mr. Ball's reckoning, when Andy exploded—and he would—the result would be a crater and a mist of lonely atoms free at last from the incessant tug of one another.

The opposing theory was presented by Miss Florentine,

the art and sometimes music and sometimes but rarely human sexuality teacher, whose interpretation was somewhat rosier. Under the school's two district championship banners, both won before any of us were born, Miss Florentine announced that Andy's sunny pallor was not a sign that his body was moving apart, but, rather, that it was moving forward. What we were witnessing, she explained, was a pointed, emergent evolution of the human spirit. An outspoken believer that children are God's little miracles, that children *grow*, that children *change*, Miss Florentine insisted that Andy was becoming something greater and more affirming than the sullen and, let's be honest, dark-minded boy we all knew. Yes, he would explode. But what else did one expect on the eve of a new era? Andy's explosion was just one small part of his renewal, rebirth, and reimagination. He was a prophet, she insisted, a messiah born unto mankind, erasing the original sins of *Homo sapiens sapiens* and delivering something more advanced, and exalted, and even, dare we say, *holy*? Miss Florentine thought it right that we did.

"That's not how evolution works," Mr. Ball said from behind a stern bulwark of middle school science.

"That's not how it *used* to work," said Miss Florentine.

Mr. Ball was unmoved. The simple fact was that Andy represented a threat, not only to himself but to the community as well. Imagine, he said to the assembled parents, some of whom were polite enough to look earnestly concerned, what would happen if Andy's antisocial particles weren't content with only pulling him apart. The law of conservation of matter clearly stated that Andy's rebellious quarks and gluons could be neither created nor destroyed. Did we really want them hanging around, fraternizing with other atoms in ways that might eventually mean the dismantling of our schools? The disintegration of our homes? The sudden poofy evaporation of our children? Is that what we wanted?

That is in no way what I want, parents muttered in a sudden outbreak of consensus, *and neither does my spouse. No reasonable, good-hearted American parent would want that*, was the general feeling.

Nonsense, Miss Florentine said. Anyone with eyes could see that Andy was a thundering miracle of nature. He was doing what we should all be doing, what we had been doing for millions of years before our environments became too agreeable and our hearts too complacent to even consider becoming something more. And now that one of us was finally returning to that grand mission of human improvement, where were we putting him? Was he not, at this very moment, in a dumpster? Was this scion of humanity not currently ankle-deep in sack-lunch juice and notebook-paper fringe? How had this group of, yes, reasonable and, yes, good-hearted and, gosh darn it, yes, American! parents allowed this to happen? Had we gone insane? What were we, a community of lunatics?

Parents squirmed at this. They wondered openly if the dumpster had at least been hosed down first, for heaven's sake. Before taking her seat, Miss Florentine asked politely if we wanted to bring the forward momentum of all humanity to a screeching halt, at which point it became fairly clear that no one knew what they wanted.

In response, Mr. Ball told them what science wanted: to bombard Andy with neutrons and antiprotons behind barriers of tungsten and lead, to watch him fall apart and fly to pieces, and study him. Miss Florentine, on the other hand, expressed her simple desire to see Andy emerge from his incandescent chrysalis, to marvel at his intricacies, to kneel at the foot of his superiority, and ooh, and aah, and study him.

We sat with our mothers' hands over our ears as the discourse began to shift from the erudite language of science and theology to our more recognizable school yard dialects. Andy's parents sat glazed, opening their mouths only to sip more coffee. But we, Andy's friends and colleagues, weren't paying attention to any of it. We were watching the dumpster, the way its lid occasionally rose like an eyebrow to reveal our friend, his blue eyes piercing the darkness of the bin like the headlights of an oncoming something, a barreling something, a something that could not be halted, or slowed, or made to give way.

Andy was eventually relocated to the tennis courts in Parish Park. The nets were taken down and the chain-link fences covered over with aluminum foil, which Mr. Ball insisted would protect both the park and the surrounding neighborhood from whatever Andy might be emitting. The foil had the added benefit of shielding Andy from view, and we were forbidden from seeing him, except for one day, when both Mr. Ball and Miss Florentine, acting as Andy's unofficial and still-feuding interim guardians, agreed that the boy's morale, which had been visibly circling the drain even after he'd been let out of the dumpster, was potentially affecting his condition for the worse. A week after his incarceration, they appeared at our front doors just before dinner, asking our parents if they would, in the interest of science and/or the betterment of the human species, allow their children to be taken to Parish Park, where, under the best protection available, we would be permitted to play with one Andrew Leon Wingham for no more than three-quarters of an hour.

Nothing was sugarcoated. Both teachers made it perfectly clear that the playdate involved no small amount of risk, that Andy's condition was believed to be highly unstable.

We knew our parents were mere moments from a chain of phone calls. Panicked voices could already be heard saying, *What do the two of you think? We're not letting ours go. Sure, it breaks our hearts to think of that poor kid, all alone and probably not even being fed properly, but rules are rules, a school night's a school night*, and so on until all involved felt absolved and sensible in their parenting.

We acted fast, put on our game faces, worked that time-honored magic that for eons has kept children in dessert and late-night TV. We whined, begged, and tantrummed until we won sighs and shrugs and were spirited away in the back of Mr. Ball's ancient Chevy Lumina to the place where Andy was kept.

If not for the square of darkening blue sky visible through a transparent screen above us, the tennis courts could have been the surface of the moon. The rough concrete under our feet was reflected on all sides by the foil walls, making the desolation of the landscape feel infinitely vast. The only sign of life was Andy, who by now was bleeding light from every pore, spitting out rays like a mirror ball. He shone brighter when he saw us. His smile made us squint.

"You're it," someone said.

We played well past our allotted forty-five minutes, barely noticing as night fell, the combination of Andy's glow and the reflective walls keeping the courts eternally daylit. Andy gave chase like a rogue comet. He beamed and blurred and froze us in all manner of failed escape. When Mr. Ball and Miss Florentine finally came in to collect us, Andy was half collapsed on the court floor, wheezing but triumphant, more radiant than ever. Mr. Ball stayed behind to take Andy's readings while Miss Florentine drove us home.

We were put to bed by shaken but relieved parents. Falling asleep almost instantly, we dreamed the troubled dreams of astronauts, nightmares of drifting free in starry space, slowly suffocating, or else accidentally tearing holes in our spacesuits, causing decompression, rapid expansion, and the sudden outing of insides.

Hours later, on the Parish Park tennis courts, invisible in his own blinding light, Andrew Leon Wingham closed his eyes, held his breath, and exploded.

II. The Immolation of Neighborhood Dogs

The next day, from the plywood observation deck overlooking the tennis courts, Mr. Ball and Miss Florentine contemplated Andy's metamorphosis.

He was bigger. Several times his previous boyish size, like a Volkswagen bus stood on end. And he still glowed, though not quite as he had.

Where Andy the boy had shed a white fluorescence, this Andy burned low and red, like the embers of a dying fire, embers with a vaguely human shape, articulation, and intelligence. His torso was a wall of superheated rock that seemed solid and flexible at the same time, melting and re-forming in turns to maintain its shape. The temperature sensor Mr. Ball had set up inside the court had more or less given up on its reporting, shrugging out only the occasional "E." Around Andy, steady waves of heat rippled and miraged, the surrounding air straining to hold him. Every few seconds a tongue of copper flame kicked up from his shoulders, or the top of his head, or from his chest, where a fiery heart might still beat.

Mr. Ball and Miss Florentine stood side by side, sharing a stupefied silence. At long last and far too late, they felt under-educated and ill-informed in matters of the world. Staring at a lava boy in a tinfoil-wrapped tennis court under a Tuesday sky, neither could conjure a confident next step.

But Andy's parents were done. For weeks, every tongue around them had gossiped. Every brow pitied. Their refrigerator was wall-to-wall with sympathy casseroles and lasagnas. Befuddled neighbors who hadn't known what to make of the situation instead made cookies, and brownies, and powdered lemon squares. But Mrs. Wingham's pantry, like her heart, had no more room for these condoling payloads, and a transformation that might have finally silenced a less exasperated mother helped this one to find her voice. Gifts of food would no longer be accepted. The town could find a new charity case. The Winghams were taking their molten son home.

There were protests, of course. Town government and public safety officials appeared on local news to make their sweaty, hyperventilating cases for jurisdiction. But Mr. and Mrs. Wingham were Andy's parents, which in our community still meant something, and soon enough the Wingham family was restored to its modest bi-level on Sondheim Road.

For a time, if you stood at a distance, peering over from next door or across the street, everything seemed fine at the Winghams'. The pool in the backyard had long since been drained, and Andy spent most of his time sitting in the deep end, looking calm and content. Maybe. It was difficult to tell if he had feelings. Andy's new head was an expressionless, neckless monolith slapped onto his new body, the sheer crag of his nose flanked by two deep-set eyes that burned the same blue we'd first seen in the gym. His movements remained adroit and boy-like, his flexible rock body bending like soft bread, breathing heat the way Andy's old body had breathed air.

We were once again forbidden from visiting Andy by our parents, who feared for our safety, and by Andy's parents, who feared further attention. We spied from a comfortable distance. The Hallisters' tree house a few lots away offered the best view, and with birding binoculars stolen from our mothers, we watched Andy pass the time. He did next to nothing, sitting in the deep end of the pool for hours with no outward sign of boredom or interest. Sometimes, and for no apparent reason, he would stand up, stomp over to the shallow end in a few great, thudding strides, pound his foot (Was it still a foot? Did Andy still have feet?) into the chlorine-green concrete until it cracked, then march slowly back to the deep end, his footprints smoldering behind him. Once or twice a day, Mrs. Wingham came onto the patio with a ham sandwich and potato chips on a plate in one hand and a glass of milk in the other, barely looking at Andy before setting them next to the diving board and retreating back into the house. Andy took them in his hands (hands?) and stared at them for a minute or two while the plate melted and the chips and sandwich caught fire and the glass shattered and milk spilled all over him, hissing like a skillet. He never once reacted. He didn't appear to suffer hunger or thirst. He never looked tired. If he slept or laughed or cried or spoke, we never saw it. Mrs. Wingham never returned for the dishes. Before long she was bringing the sandwiches out on paper napkins and pouring the milk straight into the ground.

After weeks of watching from a distance, and deep under the influence of a spring so close to summer that our only thoughts were of escape, we became staunch advocates for a free and independent Andy. The plan was to covertly remove planks from the Winghams' fence until we had cleared a large enough gap for him to walk through. We borrowed the tools we needed, and several we didn't: a dozen assorted hammers and screwdrivers, an irresponsibly sharp hacksaw, two cordless drills with whirring triggers, a half-full can of WD-40 with attached drooping red proboscis for easy spot-spraying, a complete set of socket wrenches, and a miraculously unattended oxyacetylene welding torch that none of us knew how to use. When he heard us at the base of the fence, scratching at our first picket like raccoons, Andy climbed out of the pool and came at us, plowing through the barrier almost before we could roll out of the way.

His skin crackled and fumed. Standing amid blackened slivers of fence, Andy looked to the patio door for signs of his mother, and we suddenly realized how wrong we were to think that he no longer had feelings, or that they couldn't be read. The blue flames of his eyes stared for minutes at the patio door, and in their low burn we could see Andy's caution, his concern, his hope that an adult might appear to rescue him from his rescuers, but nothing. Not even a face in the window.

Everything we had known about Andy was now obsolete. Gone was the grade-schooler who struggled with fractions and pop-tops, the playground vigilante who knew how to punch from the hips and not feel bad after, the boy teetering on the edge of goodness and badness in a childhood that seemed to him, as it did to all of us, like a never-ending negotiation of greater and lesser evils. That Andy had been obliterated, and with him any limits that had held his will to destroy in check. Now nothing was beyond his subjugation. All burned and boiled at his touch, as torments once reserved for smaller creatures, insects, worms, and the occasional bird, now found their way up the food chain. We watched as Andy cornered rabbits and squirrels against property walls, setting legs and heads and little tails aflame with barely a touch. The first frog Andy caught by the creek burst with a *plorp*, and in minutes we were lobbing frogs at him, onto his shoulders or his chest, where they would hop off on burning legs, or else stick to him, their skin going runny and splitting wide like microwaved franks until they were just more smoldering Andy, or more of the burned nothing he left behind. The strongest things we could find, steel shovels and concrete blocks and the unbendable frames of our bicycles, all melted in the brazier that was our friend. We weren't prepared for any of it, and when he trapped the Andersons' once terrifying Rottweiler in the oven of his palm, holding it against the grass as it burned and bayed like a distressed damsel, we knew there was nothing left he couldn't do, and that we could never again invite him over to play with our dogs, or spend the night at our houses, because we liked our dogs, and we liked our houses, and no amount of watching lizards cook in Andy's mouth was going to change that. Months earlier, we had all looked on in gleeful horror as Sunflower, the class guinea pig, ate two of her five wormy new offspring right in front of us. She was the hero of our hearts for months, her gruesome deed immortalized repeatedly in short, horrifying essays and crayoned caricatures. But no one played with her again after that, and eventually they took her away.

It was around lunchtime that we first noticed Mr. Ball and his sign. We were playing mouse baseball with Andy in the sandlot behind Lyman's pharmacy. A good-size mouse could be hurled from the pitcher's mound straight over the plate, where Andy would squat like a catcher, waiting for batterless strikes that shrieked and sizzled when he caught them. After a few innings, someone noticed Mr. Ball standing in the Lyman's parking lot, unshaven and hollow-faced, holding a sign. The science teacher was not daunted in his belief in Andy's inevitable dissolution, nor had he retreated from his apocalyptic warnings, which were now scrawled protest-style across a sign he was holding high. "MAKE NO MISTAKE," it read in bold capitals, "THE BOY WILL EXPLODE." Andy saw it, sprang from his catcher's squat, and ran.

We relocated a dozen or more times that afternoon, settling in whatever new parking lot or field or yard Andy chose until Mr. Ball found us in the Lumina, upon which he'd graffitied "ENTROPY IS A UNIVERSAL CONSTANT" on one side and "THIS COHESION IS FLEETING" on the other. He never spoke or acknowledged anyone but Andy, whose jerky escapes and unsteady flaring made it clear that Mr. Ball represented some kind of threat. We thought about engaging, about hurling insults and dirt clods and the grilled mice we'd saved as souvenirs, but Mr. Ball was still a teacher, and that still meant something.

Eventually we returned Andy to the Winghams' backyard. Beside the pool, a happy line of ants marched toward a puddle of sour milk and a graying tuna sandwich. Mr. Ball parked the Lumina in front of the house and stationed himself just outside the backyard fence, where he stayed the entire night, his sign looming high just over Andy's head, which is what we think eventually drove Andy out of the concrete pool that night, and into his parents' home.

Those who, prohibited by distance or deep sleep, weren't initially drawn to the scene at the sound of crumbling walls and fire engines, might still have been able to assemble the evening's events by peering through what had once been the Winghams' patio door and tracing an unobstructed path of curled linoleum and charred original wood flooring all the way back to the boy's former bedroom, where Andy could still be found (because who could have moved him?) huddled in fear, possibly of Mr. Ball, or the firemen's hoses, or the hoarse wailing of his mother, who was finally shedding all of her illusions on the Winghams' front lawn.

Once again, the issue of Andy's custody arose, but this time no one wanted him. The municipal government refused to accept responsibility for him, but admitted that his parents were hardly in a position to care for him either. Word of the proceedings also unsilenced several neighbors, who had been keeping their peace for the Winghams' sake, but now reported a number of pets who had gone, if not entirely, then at least partially missing, the cauterized remains of those few who'd hobbled home leaving little doubt as to the identity of the culprit.

The judge deciding the case, in either a stroke of genius or a desperate attempt to buy herself more time, ruled that Andy be temporarily left in the custody of the fire department, which would be charged with his safekeeping until a more appropriate home could be found.

III. The Firehouse

What more appropriate home could there possibly be?

We did not know the firemen, but we knew of them. They were our friends' fathers and our fathers' friends. During the period of Andy's confinement, we were forced to deploy a covert network to gather intelligence. We eavesdropped on Friday night poker games and sat invisibly in the corners of barber shops. Our agents heard quiet confidences across the whitewashed pickets of good neighbors not normally prone to gossip. *It's really not my place*, grown men whispered as mowers idled, *and I feel for the kid, I do. But does this strike you as an appropriate use of our tax dollars?* We met regularly in the Hallister tree house to piece together what we could.

Andy was being kept in the firehouse's training yard in a structure that the firemen called the Cinderblock, four stories of concrete walls and windows and little else that the firemen sometimes set ablaze to practice ladder climbs, search-and-rescues, and long-range spray-downs. Inside, the Cinderblock looked like a burned-out elevator shaft. Windows let in a patchwork of focused sun and wind at the higher levels, but Andy required only shelter from Mr. Ball, who waited just outside the firehouse grounds, the letters of his newest apocalyptic decree still wet on the raised plywood.

The firemen naturally regarded Andy with cautious apprehension. They understood why responsibility for his care should fall to them above all others, but even so, his presence in the training yard made them constantly nervous. Always that campfire smell in the air, the alarms in their heads never going completely silent. At night, they woke at odd hours, and would have to spend a cigarette or two staring out the window at the dull, hearthy glow of the Cinderblock before their nerves settled enough to sleep.

The chief of the firehouse, a grizzled old hose jockey, was quick to spot this disquiet, and didn't care for it. He had seen hundreds of fires in his tenure, and if there was one thing he knew, it was that you couldn't beat a fire by standing across the street pointing at it. You had to get your cheeks sooty. That's how you got rid of fear.

The chief developed a new series of advanced training exercises, and recruited Andy as a key player. Andy's job was to use his burning limbs to start new fires on different faces and levels of the Cinderblock without warning. Just as the squad would gain the upper hand on one floor, a window on the opposite side of the structure would start spouting flames, demanding the redeployment of ladders and manpower. For the first time in their careers, the firemen were forced to combat an intelligent enemy, one that could learn their strategies, adapt to their tactics, and constantly test the limits of their skill.

Simply put: They were in fireman heaven.

At the end of the first day of exercises, Andy emerged from the Cinderblock to find the entire company applauding and saluting their worthy foe. As the week of training went on, Andy's participation led to a dramatic increase in the squad's overall communication, efficiency, and teamwork. At night, some of the firemen found themselves inexplicably drawn to the Cinderblock, lingering for a few moments outside its blackened walls before finally wading into the soft light of Andy's corona to contemplate his heat and the blue flicker of his eyes.

At the firemen's weekly barbecue, Andy was again the center of attention. With Andy, grilling took minutes. Bratwurst and Polish sausages sizzled instantly in his hand. The firehouse chef, a great advocate of chilies and bran, used overlong tongs to flip sirloin on Andy's lap. Those who preferred meat rare had merely to wave a fillet in his general direction. That night, drunk on beer and beef, the firemen sat around Andy in a circle to sweat off the day's calories. Under the quiet watch of moon and stars and Mr. Ball, they smoked cigarettes and cigars, sang songs, and swayed their arms in manly jubilee.

The next morning they met in the chapel for mass. The firehouse chaplain was a large man who refused to suffer the indignity of the fire pole. His sermon that day warned against the veneration of false idols. "For ours is a jealous God," he explained, "and you would be too if it was written that there was no power in the universe greater than your almighty power, and yet were forced to watch as those who had been your loyal friends and creations suddenly turned their backs on you, choosing instead, and who knows why, the Fiery Pit, which burns men totally, and without mercy."

A handful of the firemen weren't sure what to make of this sermon, which summoned a conflict that irritated the very core of their firemanly natures. But most simply knelt, still a little hungover, fingers crawling over rosary beads as they prayed to never know what it was to burn.

IV. Andy's Daughters

The Fourth of July we run amok.

The Fourth is a beer in the hand and a burger in the lap of every grown man and woman from sea to shining sea. We love it so much we light the sky on fire. We throw it a parade.

We always broke into our bags early, snatching from their gunpowdery bottoms the smoke bombs, ladyfingers, and bottle rockets that had no place beside the nighttime majesty of Roman candles, sparklers, and bombs bursting in air. Once the daylight items were burned lifeless, we begged snow cones off our parents on Prince Edward Street and waited for the parade to start.

First came the Kingfisher marching band in their plum uniforms and piped ivory hats, followed by the living remains of this war and that, followed by the fraternal brotherhoods, and the children's choirs, and the women who made quilts for needy causes. And there were balloons. Every year Kit Kirby filled the big gorilla he used for advertising off Route 7 with helium and walked it down the road by its ties, and Edna Pequil had a nylon Santa that she inflated for no particular reason, except that preschoolers, with no regard whatsoever for the province of the holiday, went crazy when they saw it. Then came Mr. Ball, the haggard, phlegmy middle of a sandwich board that read "DISSOLUTION IS IMMINENT" on its front and on its back "NOTHING SO GROSSLY POWERFUL SHOULD BE." Mute and mortally disheveled, he marched drone-like down the boulevard, and behind him, Andy followed.

We hadn't seen Andy in over a month. The firemen didn't suffer trespassers, and more than once our curiosity had been met with the business end of a fire hose. Now here he was, marching just ahead of the fire engine, which had been washed and waxed to an electric shine. He looked taller, the flaming mantel of his shoulders wider and more wildly flammable, the blue fires of his eyes occasionally flashing a strong, stony white.

Then the show began. Thunderous overhead booms that followed a little too late behind spherical bursts of gold and green never living long enough to touch the ground. Children came armed with starlight crackling on sticks, sparks of hot gold feather falling to the concrete to disappear like melting snow. The Fourth was alive, grand and dazzling, and all looked heavenward to behold it.

There was a gunfire pop closer to us. We scanned the crowd for the misfire, the joker who'd gotten reckless and possibly maimed, until our eyes fell on a chunk of flaming pitch lodged in the taillight of a nearby pickup. Both sound and stone had come from Andy.

There was a fist-size hole in his chest, a place that had once been smooth glowing rock, now a tiny cavern. Then another report, this one like a car backfiring underwater, and something dripped from Andy's hand, landing solidly on an iron manhole cover a few feet from where we stood.

It was a small piece of burning Andy, but here, separate from him, it was still alive. The rock stood upright on little legs of fire, and sprouted little arms, and made itself a little head like a burning match. In seconds, it zipped down the street, skittering between the sidewalks and mortifying a nearby flock of pigeons into flight. Then came a popcorning of small explosions as more pieces burst from Andy's bulk, or else dripped from the molten parts of him two or three at a time, each a hand of waving fingers landing on the ground with a sticky *thud* before springing up on tiny scalding feet. Andy's chest was suddenly in full eruption, and what he erupted jumped and darted through a forest of legs and lawn chairs in search of tinder.

Andy's daughters ran wild, pollinating anything remotely

flammable with plumes of fiery hair. Before anyone had sense enough to panic, the smaller shops around us began to burn, first from the outside, their quaint decorative shutters and eave-strung plastic flags catching all too quickly, then from within.

What luck that the firefighters were there.

Dressed in their best hats and coats, the rubber of their boots spotless, the polished nozzles of their hoses bright with the reflections of nascent fires, the firemen leapt from the railings of the truck. After months of battling Andy, they acted now as a single mind, one that sensed the fire all around it, not just in the walls and windows of the nearby buildings, but in the filaments of the street lamps, the stars in the sky, the sleeping hearts of the fireworks that had yet to be lit. Their hoses made great arms of water, dashing flames from the rooftops in strong, thorough swipes. Their ladders delivered them instantly to yelping survivors whom they plucked from windows like ripe fruit.

We should have been running, screaming, searching for our mothers and then diving behind them, but there was no turning away from Andy. He was an artillery shell, each glowing part of him bursting out, breaking free, and leaving less of him behind. Left with little recourse, the firemen finally turned their biggest cannons and strongest hoses on what was left of him, beating him into the concrete with all the water on earth, every gallon, every drop, until the small fires of his eyes were finally lost in a great white nimbus of steam.

When it was over, the firemen applied first aid to the wounded, looking as shaken as those they were aiding.

Though they'd been successful and unquestionably efficient, their faces were blackened by more than soot, and wet with more than hose water. Prince Edward Street was a disaster that no one wanted to leave. The wet wrapped themselves in picnic blankets. The singed sought balm and sympathy. Mr. Ball, victorious at last, sat on the curb and sobbed.

Adults moved from gaggle to gaggle, recounting what they had just witnessed as though their audience hadn't also just witnessed it, describing wild, impossible events everyone knew to be true. Open fire hydrants had turned the street into a small river, and rats flooded out of their sewers swam its currents in search of higher ground, taking refuge atop bus stop benches, parked cars, and the monument of melted rock that had once been Andy, our friend and colleague, a cairn of stones now cold to the touch.

Eventually the police started taking statements just so people would leave. Fireworks were still reporting from nearby skies, but were impossible to see under the dense canopy of smoke. After a few hours, its astonishment fully exhausted, the town wandered home.

We managed to save one of Andy's daughters for a short time.

She hopped into the mason jar we'd been using to light inch-and-a-halfers. We carried her back to the tree house wrapped in a wet flag and poked air holes in the lid with a screwdriver. The next morning, we dropped in a habitat of twigs and leaves that she burned into a bedding of ash. We managed to keep her going for a few days on a diet of Kleenex and rolled newspaper, but anyone could see she was already starting to dim, and in our hearts, we knew she wouldn't last long. Nothing kept in that way ever does.

Jenny

This is how Jenny eats:

I chew her food, then put her esophageal tube to my lips and push the warm globs of mash into it with my tongue. Jenny forces them down using a series of complicated inhales that involve her entire body. Her neck-cap, which sits on her neck exactly where her head would begin if she had one, helps her regulate the flow of air, switching between esophagus and trachea to create brief periods of suction. Her chest expands and contracts under her silk blouse in punctuated bursts that jerk her shoulders back and forth. Her tear-cut diamond necklace, last month's sweet sixteen present from Mother, bounces against her chest as she struggles with the food, the esophageal tube wet with plumbing sounds until the glob clears the neck-cap and peristalsis takes over. She always gets them down eventually. Learning to eat has been one of Jenny's more significant accomplishments. She manages almost all of it on her own, except for the chewing.

Thank you, she taps onto my palm. *More please*. Then

she taps, *Delicious!*, even though there's no way for her to taste any of it, which gives you an idea of her sense of humor.

Jenny's seat at the table is set with cutlery just like ours, all of which goes unused. No mouth ever touches her napkin. When I take bites for her, I take them from her plate, never from my own. When I first started helping Jenny eat, I would sometimes forget whose food I was chewing (it all tastes the same—she eats what we eat), and would swallow bites meant for her without thinking. It's a hard thing to get used to, chewing food without swallowing it. I would try to make up for it by chewing a bite from my own plate and putting that in her tube, but Mother always noticed. It happens again tonight, even though it hasn't in months, because I'm distracted. I'm thinking about the date I had with Joyce the night before, about how nice it was to eat next to a woman without chewing her food for her. I notice my mistake the same time Mother does. I don't need reminding, but she reminds me.

"Jenny has her own food, Douglas," she says like it's the first time, "and you have yours." As she says it, no part of her stirs. Her curled steam-white hair sits perfectly still. She holds her tone in check, her knife in midcut.

Jenny can't hear Mother, but can feel that the slight tremor of the table made by the cutting of food has stopped.

What did she say? she taps on my knee under the table so Mother can't see. I answer on her napkin-draped lap.

I accidentally ate your food again.

I don't mind, Jenny taps. *You can have some.*

She minds.

Why?
Who knows.
What are we eating?
Chicken Kiev and steamed asparagus over rice pilaf.
What makes chicken Kiev different from regular chicken?
There's some kind of butter sauce in the middle.
Is it good?
It's okay.
Give me some chicken Kiev. Tell me when it's coming.

It's coming, I tap, then press the bite I've been working on down into the tube.

Ours wasn't always a house of strict rules, but then Jenny came. She's not the first person to be born without a head, but she's the only one to have lived into her teens, and the cost of that survival, the constant vigilance required just to keep her alive through those first few years, changed all of us. Father's change was that he died. Mother said it was heartbreak, but now I know there were also pills. Mother's change was that she was never again a proud parent. Her daughter would never speak, never laugh, never be a great beauty. She would never beam with daughterly affection, or perform it in ways that others could look upon without cringing. Jenny's private love would never make up for what she cost our mother in dignity, and because there was no way for Jenny to sense how much this hurt her, she never tried to hide it. Her spine never bent again. Endurance was all she had left.

In those early days, we were told that Jenny could go at any time, that any small disturbance in care or routine might break the delicate spell of her being alive, so my change was that I became a boy who barely moved, barely spoke, would not take a breath unless it was safe to do so. And so we became a new family, the dead father, the decimated mother, the son who never breathed, and at our center, headless Jenny, who asked only that we care for her, protect her, and show her the world as we had come to know it.

This is how Jenny sleeps:

On her back, in a white cotton nightgown peppered with blue flecks, with a glass of water on her nightstand into which she can dip her esophageal tube if she wants and, in her own way, suck. If she needs help, there's a button set into the wall next to her headboard she can press, and "The Bells of St. Mary's" will ring throughout the house until one of us comes. On either side of the bed are two monolithic stereo speakers, each half as tall as me, with a subwoofer the size of a small toaster oven hidden under the comforter at her feet. The CD player's carousel is stacked with old bass-heavy hip-hop and rap compilations. Artists don't matter. When she wants a new one, I just go to the 99-cent rack at the Disc 'N Vid and pick the first album I find with the word "bass" in the title. *Android Funk and the Third-Bass All-Stars*, *Return to Big Bass Country*, *The Bass That Ate Brooklyn 2: The Phat Bombs of August*. They spin like ammunition inside the machine, waiting to fire off their hard, thumping rounds. I tuck her in between the pillars of black foam, making sure that her water glass is full and within reach, and with the treble set to 0 and the bass set to 9, I let the stereo loose. The speakers purr, and I can feel the hum of the sub-woofer in my gut. The house thrums like a beehive. The walls take a soft but steady beating. Breakables millimeter their way across the shelves. It's the only way Jenny can sleep without waking in the middle of the night. In Mother's house of unnegotiable boundaries, where everyone takes responsibility for themselves and eats what's in front of them, Jenny is allowed this gift of our indulgence. Ever since she was a little girl, this has been our family's lullaby.

When I was seventeen, Mother was restocking my dresser with balls of laundered socks when she found the Sears catalog lingerie section folded up under my shorts.

Mother always addresses problems head-on. It's how we've come this far.

She called me into her sewing room, sat me down on the hassock, and set fire to the pages in an aluminum wastebasket right in front of me. We watched them burn like witches while Mother reiterated the importance of growing up to be a good, clear-minded man, and the shameful wrongness of associating bodies with pleasure. This, she explained, was the curse that came with the senses.

I only half listened, trying instead to commit the pages to memory as they curled and smoked, to capture the contours of each supple curve and frank, open navel before it charred and disintegrated. Alone in my room, I can still conjure those bodies sometimes, the way their skin blushed at the touch of Mother's lit match, the glow crawling over every inch of them, chewing at them in that way that fire twists and darkens but never fully erases.

This is how Jenny and I walk to the pharmacy:

Carefully, with poise and control, so that the difficulty of the task is never fully apparent to onlookers, which is everyone. Jenny walks tall in boots borrowed from Mother's closet. She has every reason to. Below her neck-cap, she has the body and bearing of a self-assured, sophisticated young woman. Her outfit is conservative, but flattering. She has Mother's strong spine. "Shame" isn't a word we use around Jenny. We purposefully don't have a tap for it. It's a feeling Mother has excised from Jenny's vocabulary and, thus, her experience. She doesn't feel the city watching her without fear of retaliation. She has no idea how defenseless she is. On these trips, I'm meant to look out for her, to keep her out of trouble, but there's no hiding our two bodies, our one head. Every living creature slows to stare. People shudder. Children can't help themselves. Dogs are curious. There's nothing I can do but receive every single stinging eye.

We wander into the restoration of an old apartment building spilling out onto the sidewalk, stopping so Jenny can examine it, which she does whenever we encounter something unexpected on our usual route. Deviations from the norm fascinate her, and their investigation is something

Mother encourages. I monitor as Jenny fondles traffic cones and follows yellow caution tape with her small, methodical hands. She runs her fingers along the scaffolding and struts, quietly mapping the bracing angles, the pleats of her skirt folding and unfolding in the wind tunnel of a covered walkway built to protect pedestrians from falling plaster and shards of lime. Her exploration is a slow, focused ritual. She leans and bends, gripping every pole, touching every bolt, stretching out our time away from home as much as she can. This world, overflowing with newness, is what she wants.

What does this sign say?

Ha-ha.

What?

It says watch your head.

Ha-ha. That's funny.

We're walking to the pharmacy to restock Jenny's battery of medication, and to see Joyce, and to buy, if Jenny is good (Mother's words, not mine), a new emery board, a new pair of clippers, and a new bottle of polish to feed Jenny's fanatical preoccupation with her nails. She's holding my hand in both of hers, tapping into it as we walk.

Are you going to ask Joyce out again?

I don't know. Maybe.

On a date?

Maybe.

How was your last date with her?

I told you.

Tell me again.

It was pretty nice. We had dinner and played mini golf.

And how was the date before that? Jenny makes it sound like this sort of thing happens all the time.

It was pretty nice, too.

And how was the date before that?

There aren't any before that. We've only had two dates.

Ha-ha. I know. Did you kiss her?

Not yet. You asked me that yesterday.

Ha-ha. I know. Do you love her?

Not yet, I don't think.

Where will you take her on your date?

I don't know.

Out for chicken Kiev?

Maybe.

Delicious!

The pharmacy isn't busy, which is good. Joyce is behind the counter. She sees us coming and squints as she smiles, which I get the feeling she can't help. She's really something, though. Slim—there's almost nothing to her—with orange curls that she keeps bundled up with pins and soft freckled skin. She does have these sort of puffy sacs under her eyes, and the squinting bunches them up and makes them kind of worse, but she's got full, seriously great lips. I lead Jenny up to the counter and place her hands on the glass. Joyce and I do our hellos.

Tell her I say hello.

"It's nice to see you today," Joyce says to Jenny slowly, working her way around the vowels, and again I wonder if she really understands Jenny's condition, or if she thinks that being headless is like being hard of hearing.

Tell her I say hello.

I tell Joyce that Jenny says hello.

"Did you tell her that I said hello, too?" she asks. I tell her I did, and then I do, and Jenny taps hello again, and for a few moments we chat like this, politely out of sync. Then Jenny squeezes my hand and says she wants to go find some nail polish. It's a few aisles into the store, but she's made the walk plenty of times by herself, feeling her way along until her fingers locate the bottles, which she'll work through slowly until she finds one with a shape and weight she likes. The color doesn't matter. She doesn't wear it for other people. I let her go.

I hand Joyce a bag full of Jenny's empty prescription bottles, and she hands them to a small, sad-looking pharmacist behind her. Then she turns back toward me and I start to ask her out, but before I can finish, she breaks up with me.

"Doug," she says, crumpling her mouth into a fret, "I'm just not sure we should keep seeing each other like this." That's how she says it, and I'm wondering what she means by "like this," so I ask her.

"I just don't think starting a relationship is healthy for two people in our situation," she says, "with me as, you know, an employee here, and you being a customer. Plus your sister's condition and all. I guess I just don't think it's for the best. I can't see it working out in a way that, in the end, we can all feel comfortable with, so maybe it's better if we just call the whole thing off now, before anyone gets hurt, and while we're still such good friends."

I ask her why she suddenly feels this way.

"Oh, I don't know," she says, letting her shoulders sink. "This is so hard. I think I just didn't ever really imagine this would be something long-term. Because, I mean, did *you* ever really think this was going to turn into something, I guess, real? Because I thought we were just having some friendly fun. We needed to get you out there, to get a few dates under your belt, and so we did. And so now I just think, well, so, we did it. It's done."

I ask her what she means. Then I ask her if going out with me was some sort of charity thing. If that's what all this was.

"No, God, Doug. It's just that when you first asked me out I thought—"

Because I don't need her charity.

"That's not what I—"

Because if that's the idea, I want to tell her, she can forget it. I want to tell her that if that's the idea, to hell with it and to hell with her. Jenny may need people's charity, but I don't. That's the difference between us. I want to make Joyce acknowledge that Jenny and I are separate people with separate lives, and that with her puffy eyes and her weird squinty-smile thing, she's in no position to be taking pity on anybody, but in the end I don't get the chance, because just then one of the other customers rushes over to the counter and tells us that Jenny's been assaulted.

It's impossible to tell if the officer taking our statements is uncomfortable because of Jenny or because of what's happened to her. I don't know what the normal procedure is following a sexual assault, but I'm guessing stammering and no eye contact aren't part of the protocol.

Jenny taps her version of what happened into Mother's palm. She is calm. Calmer than the officer, and me, and Mother, who, after years of taking her outrageous misfortune in stride, is finally caving in right in front of us, barely able to translate as Jenny describes a body behind her, followed by a warm, open-palmed hand under her skirt. She describes two fingers and a thumb on the right side of her hip, and so, she thinks, the left hand of a left-handed person. She recounts a long moment of firm, steady pressure between her legs, and then nothing. Jenny taps the words. Mother makes the report. The officer asks questions, which mother must then translate to daughter.

Did it go—Mother has to pause—*sweetie, in? My dearest, did they go*—she pauses again, holds her breath—*in you?*

Maybe a little. Jenny thinks about it. *Why?*

The answer breaks Mother. The officer does his best. He is part of us now. Just by being here, by taking the notes, he is one of our small circle of constant, perpetual victimhood.

"Who?" Mother asks. "Who? What kind of creature could?" But I know better. We can't help our attractions, our desires. Even now, I want Joyce. At the pharmacy, she'd cried as they'd questioned her, her eyes red, their puffy underbellies slick and rosy as she told the officer how much she wished she could have done something, prevented it somehow. She told him how sweet Jenny was, how obviously innocent, as if either of these things were in question. She made the same sniffling, gasping sounds that Mother is making now, and even then, with her face blotched and tearful and her makeup crawling down her cheeks, I wanted her.

Mother blames me.

"I blame you, Douglas," she tells me as I drive the three of us home. She doesn't mince words. Someone has exploited a chink in her armor, and that chink, she tells me, is me.

"You're the chink in my armor, Douglas," she says. "You let them stab me in the heart." She repeats it every few blocks until we pull into the drive.

That night I find Jenny in my room, investigating. She can be a real snoop sometimes. She's found the earplugs I keep in a little pouch next to my bed for when the hum of the walls becomes too much. She's rolling them between her fingers, testing their sponginess, feeling them give and re-form. I take her hand.

It's time for bed.

What are these?

Nothing. Earplugs. We put them in our ears to keep sound from getting in.

They're funny.

They're nothing.

What do you need them for? Is it noisy where we live?

I can't stand to look at her. I take her other hand, pressing the earplugs between our palms.

I'm tired, I tap. *It's time for bed.*

Okay. Good night.

182

She lets go of one hand, but I hold on to the other.

What is it?

I don't know.

What is it?

Did it hurt?

What?

Did he hurt you?

I don't know. It felt strange. It felt funny. I didn't know what was happening. At first, I thought it was you.

Me?

I knew it wasn't you. His hands were too big. But he was gentle and scared, the way you are sometimes. He was nervous, the way you were before you talked to Joyce. That's all.

I'm sorry.

It's okay. Are you going out with Joyce again?

I'm so sorry.

It's okay. Are you going out with Joyce again? Did you ask her out again?

Yes.

Another date?

Yes.

Chicken Kiev?

Yes.

Delicious!

Yes. Delicious.

Ha-ha. Good night.

Her other hand slips away.

The next morning Mother makes what Jenny claims is her favorite breakfast, eggs Benedict and cinnamon toast, which is fine, even though hollandaise tastes like Elmer's glue to me. At the table, Mother tells me I have to take Jenny back to the police station. She's received an early-morning call. They have a suspect in custody. This seems soon to me, but apparently they got a good look at the guy from the pharmacy's security camera, which has helped them make a quick collar.

"I just don't think I can go back there, Douglas," Mother says in a way that makes it clear she won't.

Then, so there's no confusion: "I won't go back to that place."

What did she say? Jenny asks after sucking down a yellowish glob.

We have to go back to the police station, I tap on her palm above the table, making sure Mother can see. *Just you and me.*

Okay, she says. Mother glares. Jenny dips her esophageal tube into her orange juice glass and drains it dry.

The policemen are nervous about letting Jenny feel the hands of the men in the lineup, but Jenny assures me that it's okay, so I assure them.

"Thing is, we're not sure if it'll hold up," the policeman from the night before says. "Legally, I mean. It's not exactly procedure," and I nod like I understand, though I'm not sure what else they expect Jenny to do with a lineup. I tell him that if it's the guy, she'll know it, which is the truth. Jenny remembers hands like most people remember faces. A handshake is all she needs to know who she's talking to. She loves meeting new people.

The police seem eager to make an arrest. They want this whole thing over with as much as we do. The officer leads Jenny into the room where the men are lined up. I watch from behind the glass.

The men are ordered to hold out their left hands, palms up. Jenny takes them one by one, examining them with her usual patience.

They stare at her with the looks we're used to. Some reel at her touch, craning away as much as they can. Most focus on her neck-cap, their natural reaction being to look to where her head should be, to the part of her that should be reassuring them that all is well, that she means them no harm.

One near the end of the line doesn't seem as bothered by her. He gives his hand over to her inspection without any fear that I can see. All of the men are oldish and squat with thinning hair, similar to one another in the way lineups are required to be for the sighted, but this man has a stockier build than the rest. Blue tattoos peek out from under thatches of white hair on his forearms. He doesn't look at Jenny's neck-cap, but instead at his hand in hers, watching as she charts the network of his palms, the segments of his digits, the shape and cut of his nails. Jenny lingers on this hand, going over it again and again. She seems unable to make up her mind about something, and there is a terrible moment where I think she might put his hand between her legs to be sure, but then she lets go and moves on to the next man's waiting hand. After she's examined them all, the officer leads her back behind the glass and she takes my hand in hers.

Tell them he's not here.

Are you sure?

Yes. Tell them he's not here.

They said they got a good look at him on the camera, I tell her. *They said they think they've got him.*

Tell them he's not here.

I tell the officer.

"Is she sure?"

I tell them she seems pretty sure.

"Does she want to take more time? She can go through them again if she wants."

Let's go to the pharmacy, she taps.

They want to know if you want to go through them again.

Why?

To be sure.

I am sure. Tell them he's not here. Let's go to the pharmacy.

I tell the officer that she's sure, that we're done. The sides of his mouth bunch. He tells the men in the lineup through an intercom that they're dismissed.

On the drive home Jenny is still insisting that we go to the pharmacy. She has yet to receive the nail polish she was promised yesterday.

And you can talk to Joyce about your date.

I don't think we should go.

Why not?

I don't think it's a good place to go right now. I don't think we should go back there.

Why?

I can't believe you want to go back there.

Don't you want to see Joyce?

No.

You can talk about your next date.

We're not going on another date.

Why not?

She doesn't want to see me anymore.

Why not?

Because she doesn't.

Why not?

Because she said she doesn't.

You said she did.

I don't respond.

You said she did.

My hand sits limply in hers, like a dead animal she's trying to prod back to life. I concentrate on driving. The car wants to stray. It's easing away from the yellow line. It might be the crosswind, or the alignment. It's hard to keep steady with one hand.

Why did you say she did?

I can't say what I want to say. We don't have a tap for it.

Why did you—

I pull away from Jenny and take hold of the wheel with both

hands in order to drive properly. I drive like this the whole way home, hands at ten and two, like Mother taught me.

It's late, and I'm awake in bed. I can feel the hum of Jenny's sound system in my teeth. I think of her attacker, still out there, still walking free, still suffering under the curse that comes with the senses.

She has to know that it's my fault. She should say so. She should know. I want to tell her how angry she should be. I want to tell her that things will never be the same for her again, that she'll never feel safe now because she'll never know for sure if I'm there or if I'm somewhere else, not thinking of her or the danger she's in, which is out there, and real, and constant. I want to tell her to turn down the god-damn bass, that it's keeping us awake and shaking the whole goddamn house down. I want to tell her that her world has been shattered, that she can never go back, and then maybe I'll tell her what a sorry, pitiful creature she is, and how fucking unbearably pitiful she makes us. I want to tell her how fucked my life is because of how fucked her life is. These are the things I am going to tell her, right now in the middle of the night. These are the things she should know.

This is how I find her:

Writhing, bedsheets kicked aside, bass pulsing through the room like an intoxicated brain, the tower speakers thumping themselves into a blur, the subwoofer quaking like a frightened animal as she cradles it with her hands, burying it deep between her thighs, pressing it hard against the folds of her nightgown, her esophageal tube slowly sliding left to right as her hips buck awkwardly against the rhythm. Jenny lets the hard, solid tones beat against her. Her fingers, those slender daisies, struggle to keep the woofer nestled in place. She cleaves to it with knees and nails. Her hands are steady, practiced, like she's done this before. Her water glass, nudged by waves of sound, inches closer and closer to the edge of the nightstand with each beat until it falls onto the bed, spilling out onto the sheets and onto Jenny before rolling off and shattering. Jenny must sense the spill, but doesn't stop. I don't know if she can feel me watching, or if she would even care. I wonder if Mother has explained to her the wrongness of associating bodies with pleasure. I wonder if Jenny thinks touch and love are the same thing. She tightens her grip on the subwoofer. Her thighs are quivering and bare. A sudden shoulder jerk whips her esophageal tube against the wall, smacking the call button dead center. "The Bells of St. Mary's" chimes angelically above the beat. Mother, if she is awake, is on her way.

I leave the room quickly and close Jenny's door behind me, the lullaby still coursing inside. Mother is already halfway down the hall. She's tying her robe around her, squinting and maybe still half asleep.

"What happened?" she asks.

"Her water glass fell off the nightstand."

"I'll get a broom" she says.

"I'll take care of it," I say. "Go back to bed."

"I'll just check on her then."

"She's fine," I say, still in front of the door. "I'll take care of it."

Mother looks at me with one eye still asquint, unsure if I'm being stubborn or helpful. She rewraps her robe around her. It's oversize, and might have been my father's. It keeps trying to swallow her up.

The beat drops, then rebounds, then skids backward into a crescendo. Behind me, the door struggles against the jamb. Mother, unable to find an easy way into Jenny's room, pretends not to want one, retreating down the hall with no good night.

Here is your armor, Mother. Here is your good, clear-minded son.

I wait in front of Jenny's door until Mother's closes, and then for another hour after that, until all of our bodies are still together. Jenny's lullaby plays all night. I stay put. I take almost no breaths. Still though, I'm here.

Rite of Baptism

Officiant: What name do you give your child?

Parents: [Name].

Officiant: And what do you ask of the Church for [name]?

Parents: Baptism.

Officiant: You have asked to have your child baptized. In doing so, you are accepting the responsibility of guiding [him/her] down the River, through its sluicing corridors and over its gulping rapids. It will be your duty to keep [name]'s head above water, [his/her] pate dry, [his/her] little nostrils clear, and [his/her] little toes unmuddied. Do you clearly understand what you are undertaking?

Parents: We do.

Officiant: But do you really?

Parents: Totally.

Officiant: Godparents, are you prepared to help [name]'s parents as they guide [him/her] down the River? Are you prepared to keep [name]'s crèche afloat, to ward off, as much as possible, the many perils of the River, for example, the ravenous hippos and crocodiles, the apes with semihuman intelligence, and the creatures that appear to be otters, but are more menacing than otters, as evidenced by their tendency to bite? And, if necessary, are you prepared to pull the body of the nearly drowned, otter-bitten [name] from the baleful current of the River and perform CPR, keeping in mind that, when performing CPR on an infant, one should use only two or three fingers to apply chest compressions at a rate of approximately one hundred compressions per minute?

Godparents: We are.

Officiant: [Name], the Church welcomes you with great joy and claims you in the name of the Lord of the River. I now invite your parents to place you in your crèche, which they have fashioned out of a collection of pliable synthetic twigs and briars from the craft bin, meant to represent, in its own crude way, the crèche of Our Lord, fashioned by His own doubtlessly loving but almost adorably naïve mother and father out of actual twigs and briars collected from the banks of the River.

[Parents place child in crèche.]

Officiant: We now ask [name]'s parents to place the crèche into the Baptismal Canal, which stretches the length of the Church, representing the River into which Our Lord was once placed by the same almost certainly loving but again—it must be said—rather dim parents, but also representing the same River into which we all arrive, be it in a crèche, or lashed to a log, or tied to a bundle of smooth river stones, the ballast of which we might struggle against our entire lives, forever aching and gasping for breath. I also invite [name]'s godparents to place into the crèche a sleeve of saltine crackers, as a reminder of the crackers placed in the crèche of Our Lord by His parents, and as a representation of the minor affordances and occasional kindnesses that we might receive on our journey down the River.

[Parents place crèche in Baptismal Canal. Godparents place sleeve of saltines in crèche.]

Officiant: [Name], as you travel down the first few bends of the Baptismal Canal, I invite your brothers and sisters, your cousins, and all of the children gathered here today to place their hands in the water of the canal and splash you a little bit, just a little bit, to represent the small torments that one encounters while navigating the River; the whirl of its eddies, the snag of its drooping branches, the mocking of its water fowl. I would also ask some of the children to submerge their arms up to the elbow and make small serpentine motions—yes, just like that— to represent the vipers and eels of the River, which wait just below the surface, looking for an unattended limb or a twiddling finger to latch on to and drag under. Parents and godparents, do you understand the predatory nature of the River's many shallow lurkers?

Parents and Godparents: We do.

[Acolytes distribute water pistols filled with imitation ape urine to older members of congregation.]

Officiant: Now, as the Baptismal Canal winds its way between pews and folding chairs, I invite the older members of our community to look upon [name] disapprovingly, as the apes with semihuman intelligence once looked upon Our Lord from their treetops above the River, where they sneered simian sneers and took turns urinating into His crèche, jealous, perhaps, of the sleeve of saltines, or the untroubled ease of His passage. As we bring to bear these plastic water pistols filled with imitation ape urine and squirt [name] as Our Lord was squirted, we recall those times when we were urinated upon, figuratively speaking, by the many sneering apes of the world, and how this wasn't so bad in the long run. How we survived being urinated upon, realizing, as [name] inevitably will, that being urinated upon is part of being on the River. Parents and godparents, do you recall being figuratively urinated upon by your own version of the apes, whatever that might be?

Parents and Godparents: We sure do.

Officiant: And did you survive it?

Parents and Godparents: Ultimately, yes, we did.

Officiant: [Name], as you float down the River in a small pool of imitation ape urine, know that the dampness is only temporary, that the smell of ape urine fades, that the insults of the apes are but one moment on the River. Remember that the River is long, and wide, and gets worse.

[Congregation meditates on this. Officiant and acolytes remove their vestments and don hard hats and reflective vests. Acolytes begin operating whirring blades.]

Officiant: As [name] now floats silently down the Baptismal Canal, past the emergency exit and the wicker shrines erected to Our Lady of Baffled Wonder, we recall Our Lord's encounter with the Sawmill, activating the whirring blades and lighting the trash fires to remind us of the industrial perils of the River. We also point the PA system directly at [name] as [he/she] bobs between the miniature cranes and smokestacks, playing a recording of Sawmill sounds at maximum volume to remind us of how loud the actual Sawmill must have been, how it must have rustled the water and shaken Our Lord's infant resolve.

[PA system plays Sawmill sounds at full hork. Acolytes direct whirring blades alarmingly close to crèche.]

Officiant (bellowing over PA): [NAME], AS YOUR EYES WATER AT THE SMOKE AND SMELL OF BURNING GARBAGE, RECALL THE TEARS OUR LORD MUST HAVE SHED AS HE LOOKED UPON THE SAWMILL, WITH ITS SMOKEFUL CHIMNEYS AND RAINBOW-SLICK WATER. WE NOW SPRINKLE SAWDUST INTO YOUR CRÈCHE AS A REMINDER THAT NOT EVERY BREATH ON THE RIVER IS A CLEAN LUNGFUL. AS YOU WINCE AT THE SAWDUST IN YOUR EYES, OR THE WHIRRING BLADES PASSING WITHIN INCHES

OF YOUR FACE, RECALL HOW OUR LORD MUST HAVE WINCED AT THE SIGHT OF THIS DULL AND TAINTED STRETCH OF THE RIVER, AND AT THE CRIPPLED AND DISFIGURED WORKMEN, WHO SURELY PUZZLED OVER HIM, SAYING:

[Acolytes each slip one arm from its sleeve to suggest maiming.]

Acolytes: WE ARE PUZZLED. WE ARE PUZZLED. WE ARE PUZZLED BY THIS CHILD. WHO IS THIS CHILD? WHO WOULD WILLINGLY FLOAT A CHILD DOWN THIS DULL AND TAINTED STRETCH OF RIVER? LOOK AT WHAT WORKING IN THIS SAW-MILL ALONG THE RIVER HAS DONE TO US. COUNT OUR MISSING FINGERS, OUR SUBTRACTED LIMBS. OBSERVE THE GROSSNESS OOZING FROM THE DRAINAGE PIPE, WHICH GATHERS ON THE SUR-FACE OF THE WATER LIKE SOUP SKIN. BREATHE THIS HORRIBLE AIR. WHAT MANNER OF PARENTS WOULD SET A CHILD UPON THIS COURSE? HOW ALMOST ADORABLY NAÏVE THEY MUST HAVE BEEN TO DO SUCH A THING!

Officiant: PARENTS AND GODPARENTS, DO YOU RE-ALIZE THE INDUSTRIAL PERILS TO WHICH YOU HAVE EXPOSED [NAME] SIMPLY BY BRINGING [HIM/HER] HERE AND SETTING [HIM/HER] UPON THE COURSE OF THE RIVER?

Parents and Godparents: We do.
Officiant: SPEAK UP, PLEASE.
Parents and Godparents: SORRY. YES, WE DO.

[Congregation meditates on this. PA system is turned off. Officiant and acolytes remove reflective vests and hard hats. Acolyte posing as Child's Secret Enemy, masked and wearing turtle shell, approaches Baptismal Canal.]

Officiant: [Name], as you leave the Sawmill, drifting farther down the Baptismal Canal, out of the Church proper and into the hallway near the restrooms, we ask that you keep in mind that not all perils of the River are easily recognizable. Recall now how Our Lord encountered the Spiteful Turtle, His Secret Enemy, who pretended at first to be His pal, paddling alongside Him and singing the ridiculous songs of the river turtles, only to later capsize His crèche for no apparent reason.

[Secret Enemy caresses child's chin with forefinger in transparently false act of fondness and security.]

Secret Enemy (singing):

Loo-de-loo, loo-de-loll, river turtles are so small
Loo-de-lim, loo-de-leek, river turtles feel so weak
Loo-de-loo, loo-de-lie, river turtles can't say why
Loo-de-lim, loo-de-lutz, river turtles hate your guts

[Child's Secret Enemy rocks crèche, first soothingly, then stormily, then hatefully. Crèche takes on water. Child should cry anxious and/or terrified cries between gasps for air. Parents and godparents should regret everything.]

Officiant: Parents and godparents, do you regret everything you have done to [name] in bringing [him/her] here today and leaving [him/her] at the mercy of strangers and confusing, perilous rituals?

Parents and Godparents: We do. We are up to our ears in regret.

Officiant: And do you shudder to realize that, through the gatehouse and the barbican, near the entrance to the parking lot, the Baptismal Canal will empty out into the rushing torrent of the honest-to-God River, depositing [name] into the very real perils that this ritual has heretofore only simulated?

Parents and Godparents: We do. Oh God, we do. We are literally shuddering.

[Crèche follows Baptismal Canal out Church door, through gatehouse and barbican, into raging storm outside. Sharpshooters on parapets overlooking Baptismal Canal paint crèche with laser sights until child is covered in a quivering red pox. Congregation dons rain slickers and ascends stairs to parapets overlooking Canal, rubber-belted Inclined Conveyor, and honest-to-God River beyond. Rain falls as it always has. Thunder cascades across a gray world, intimating a general lack of sanctuary. Congregation meditates on this.]

Officiant: [Name], you are outside the walls and battlements of the Church, and have been targeted by those with the power to destroy you, just as Our Lord of the River was targeted by those who found His teachings reckless, misguided, and needlessly cruel. But what else was He to learn on His infant journey? What is the chief lesson of the River, if not needless cruelty? For example, look at you now, [name]. Your crèche is rain-soaked, and sawdust-soaked, and ape-urine-soaked. You are alone, desperate, panicked. What can you do? Parents and godparents, what can you offer [name]?

Parents and Godparents: We have given the child a sleeve of saltines. What more would you have us do?

Officiant: Assembled brothers and sisters, is there anything you can do for [name]?

Congregation: From this parapet, we can but watch in dumb horror.

Officiant: [Name]'s Secret Enemy, how close are you to [name]?

Secret Enemy: Even atop these battlements, I am so close, and growing closer. Close enough to smell ape urine. Close enough to smell [name]'s name. I am always just a few bends behind you, [name], for I am driven by a wild jealousy that even I don't fully understand.

[Crèche approaches Inclined Conveyor.]

Officiant: [Name], know that it was here, when all seemed lost, that Our Lord of the River chose to become a Famous Celebrity.

[Crèche enters Inclined Conveyor, begins to ascend.]

Officiant: Why did He choose to become a Famous Celebrity? How did He manage it? What does a celebrity even look like? We cannot say. The world is so much darker, and the celebrities who once littered our skies are more distant from us now than they ever were. We cannot make you a Famous Celebrity, little [name]. We do not know the secret. We cannot even tell you where to begin, except to tell you to begin at the River. But we can raise you heavenward for a brief moment before giving you to the River, that you might know what it is to see the world shrink beneath you, as Our Lord did when He ascended the gilded ranks of fame and fortune and left this doomed world behind.

[Crèche ascends.]

Congregation: We are smaller. We are smaller. We are like ants.
Officiant: Why do we tell [name] this story, and why in this way? How else might we tell it?
Congregation: How? How?

[Crèche ascends.]

Officiant: Here's how: One day a man and a woman, for reasons they never bothered to explain to anybody, put a baby into a river, wherein it listened poorly, learned poorly, and made mostly poor decisions until it died. But there's nothing to be gleaned from that account, no way to make it meaningful. It's a sad, empty story. It needs a better hero. Plus danger and excitement. Mystery and ritual. Hope spitting in the dumb donkey face of an inexplicable and indiscriminate evil.

[Crèche ascends.]

Officiant: And look around you, [name]. As you approach the apex of the Inclined Conveyor, look at this roiling maelstrom, these wind-warped trees, these angry roadkill-lined streets ripe with faunal decay. We must have meaning in a world like this, [name]. As you teeter at the Inclined Conveyor's precipice, look to the River below.

Congregation: Look! Look!

Officiant: It is a swallowing River, [name].

Congregation: Loo-de-lim, loo-de-leek!

Officiant: A devouring River.

Congregation: Loo-de-loo, loo-de-lie!

Officiant: Feel it dragging you forward, [name], pulling you in, like the baited hook at the end of the—

Congregation: WHEEEEEEEEEE!!!!!

[Crèche slides down what remains of Baptismal Canal into River, landing with a cannonball-esque sploosh. Along River, apes with semihuman intelligence should already be sneering, Sawmill furnaces already smoking, sort-of-otters already bobbing in dagger-toothed flotillas. Crèche should surface. Crèche usually surfaces.]

Officiant: Brothers and sisters, the Rite of Baptism is complete. I now invite the parents and godparents to leave the safety of the battlements and run breathlessly toward [name]'s point of impact. Trust that our sharpshooters will do their best to cover you while you attempt to rescue [name] from the River. As you do, remember that, metaphorically speaking, there is no rescuing [name] from the River, just as there is no rescuing anyone, which makes the lack of rescuing bearable, and beautiful, and forgivable. Amen.

Congregation: Amen.

[Parents and godparents descend battlements, exit gatehouse and barbican, rush to River's edge. Parents and godparents should arrive sooner than they do. Storm should howl. Parents should howl. River should course with a deep, unsolvable howling. Congregation meditates on this, descends battlements, returns to sanctuary. Hymns are hummed. Slickers are held tight. Little is said. All is forgiven.]

Blunderbuss

"W elcome! Welcome!" the time travelers say, their voices echoing through the too-spacious, too-empty lobby of the Time Travel Institute. The students, startled by the sound of adult voices, look up from the controls of the lunar rover, and down from their ascent of the stegosaurus skeleton, cautious, unsure.

"No, no," the time travelers insist, "don't stop. That's why we have that stuff. That's why it's here in the lobby. For climbing and roving! Take your time. Take turns, and when you've all had a good climb and a good rove, we'll go into the conference room and start our day."

The students, third graders all, resume their play. They are unimpressed by the words "conference room," which don't sound nearly as exciting as a life-size climbable dinosaur skeleton, or a rover that really roves. If allowed, they would never leave the lobby. All of time could empty itself onto the floor, and still they would pound against the back doors of history, scraping away paint and rust, demanding just a few more hours to make use of their arms and legs, to summit this prehistoric hill of bones, to run this rover into the ground.

After a while, the time travelers, in their standard-issue saggy gray jumpsuits, begin to question their commitment to the phrase "take your time," but they want the children to have an affirming extracurricular experience, to go back to their friends and parents and say what a total blast they had at the Time Travel Institute, and what good work the time travelers are doing there—what good, important, funding-worthy work. They do not want to jeopardize this report, and the rigid dictums of time travel regularly warn against meddling in the natural unfolding of events. Some things, the time travelers know, must simply be allowed to run their course.

But there is also a schedule to keep, a concatenation of discrete moments that will and must occur that has already taken a beating thanks to the unanticipated popularity of the lobby. Time travelers can get itchy about schedules.

Isn't there an adult they might appeal to? A teacher? A chaperone? The Time Travel Institute's events secretary must have been in contact with someone responsible for delivering the students at an appointed time and in an appropriate state of readiness, bodies clothed and brains eager. Surely they had not arrived by sheer providence. A bus driver, at least. Someone with a means of identification, a driver's license upon which hard dates of birth and expiration might be found. But there is no such person here in the lobby, and so, for almost a full hour and a half, during which time the children's enthusiasm and the time travelers' patience appear equally inexhaustible, there is a standoff.

In the end, biology wins. The students play long enough and hard enough to acquire an unignorable thirst.

"Do you have a water fountain?" they finally ask in exhausted huffs.

"We have better than a water fountain," the time travelers reply. "We have juice. And donut holes. In the conference room."

The students look to the conference room door, then to the stegosaurus, wiggle, consider.

They ask: "What kind of juice?"

The answer is: "All kinds. Apple and orange. Cranberry. Cran-apple and cran-orange. Grape. Grapefruit. Peach. Pineapple. Mango. Guava."

The students swoon at the selection. Their thirst compounds. They enter the conference room and drain carafe after carafe as the time travelers prepare their presentation materials and steady themselves against the twitching of their own nerves. This is the first time they've hosted a field trip of this kind, and they're not off to a great start.

The Time Travel Institute's conference room is larger than most conference rooms in most institutes. This is to accommodate the many historical artifacts on display in every corner of the room. There are other overly spacious rooms in the institute in which the hard science of time travel is performed, and the soft science of researching the hard science, and the nonscience of requesting, managing, and allocating funds to pay for the hard and soft sciences, but none of the other rooms are designed to impress like the conference room. The conference table, for instance, is an enormous slab of ancient sequoia. The number of rings from edge to center suggests that it is older by far than anything else in the conference room, which is saying something. The artifacts lining the walls are exquisitely practical: collapsible telescopes, pocket watches, spectacles, all appropriately antique-looking and resting on ornately carved wooden stands that are themselves antiques. But it is the armaments that capture the students' attention: the fanned cutlasses and taut crossbows, the crossed Mycenaean spears and Chinese qiang, the French muzzle-loading rifles and their German breech-loading descendants mounted in decorative martial columns, flanked by revolvers, and polearms, and primeval stone grenades.

The students have arranged themselves according to an inbred system. The more eager and scholarly students sit at the front of the table close to where the time travelers are setting up, while the easily distracted and generally more troublesome students sit at the far end, where adult supervision fades and hijinks thrive. The back-of-the-room students spin in their chairs, gazing at the gallery of treasures revolving cyclonically around them, wondering privately which to make a move on first, imagining which might be the easiest to handle, the most interesting, the most exhilarating. Brains unattuned to formal mathematics suddenly find themselves calculating mass, density, and, in the case of the glittering Japanese shuriken and the complete set of Venetian stilettos, velocity. Heavy items are more exciting as a rule, but smaller

ones make for easier concealment. Breaking is always com-
pelling. All the students in the room have a natural aptitude
for breaking things. It is a skill they have come to embrace,
and, in the case of these back-of-the-room students, hone.

"Okay," the time travelers say, indicating at long last their
good-to-go-ness. "Sorry for the wait. Come to think of it, I
guess we could have been setting up while you were in the
lobby. That one's on us," they say, expecting that the students will, in turn, apologize for playing too long. But this
would require a common decency the students don't appear
to have at their disposal. Clearly, a lesson in more than just
time travel is in order. But why must the time travelers be
the ones to deliver it? Why must they be the ones to insist
upon the proper respect and astonishment to which they are
so obviously entitled? The thought boggles their not incon-
siderable minds.

"Anyway, we're ready now," they tell the students. "Can
we stop all that spinning there in the back and start talking about the reason you're here today? Who knows what
we do here?" they ask, and the front-of-the-room students
are ready.

"You do time travel," they say.

"Yesssss!" the time travelers say. "Time travel! We travel
through time! Excellent. Now, who can tell us why time
travel is important?"

The students do not answer. The back-of-the-room students keep spinning. The front-of-the-roomers are quiet,
fidgety, unsure.

The time travelers do not have enough experience to

know that such silences can be common when dealing with third graders. It isn't always ignorance. Sometimes it's apathy. Or sugar. It could also be the artifacts. The eighteenth-century captain's sextant resting in the corner, for example, with its sleek nautical curves and precarious balance, is distraction incarnate. Its intricate golden quarters twinkle wildly, begging to be handled. Objects like these can easily sidetrack a third-grade class riding high on the glazed rush of a donut hole binge.

The question still hangs in the air: Why is time travel important? The answer seems simple enough to the time travelers: Time travel is important because it is the most objective way to study the unfolding of past events as they actually happened, to cut out history's middleman, with his incomplete record and his limited and often hopelessly biased perspective, and go straight to the source—history in its rawest, purest form.

This, and the answers to many other questions the time travelers are planning to ask, was outlined in a primer packet sent ahead to the school to prepare the students to participate in this part of the presentation. Had their teacher failed to cover this material? Where was this person? Why the woeful dereliction of duty? The time travelers' gray jumpsuits sag even more. In the interest of time, they answer their own question.

"Time travel is important," they say, "because it is the most objective way to study the unfolding of past events as they actually happened, to cut out history's middleman, with his incomplete record and his—" But the answer is cut short by the appearance of orange puke on the conference table.

The students are suddenly unwell. They feel queasy and light-headed. It might be from the spinning, or the fact that many of them have just consumed their weight in donut holes and juice, but probably not. These third graders are the tough, hardy sort. They've stared down Tilt-A-Whirls with truckloads of ice cream under their belts and barely loosed a hiccup, let alone painted their shirts with the full contents of their stomachs, which many of them are doing now, as their classmates yuck, and eww, and pee-yew.

"We're sick," the sick students moan.

"Yes," the time travelers sigh, "we were worried this might happen." A few more time travelers rush into the conference room with plastic buckets and wet towels, some just in time to catch blackish volleys of repeating grape juice splattering onto the carpet. Meanwhile, a few of the still-healthy back-of-the-room students are using the chaos of the moment to make a move for the sextant.

"It's the juice!" some of the students shout, only half serious. "The juice is poisoned! Don't drink the juice!"

"It's not the juice," the time travelers hush. "It's the time travel device. It's in the lab down the hall. You're just not used to being so close to it, and it's upsetting your systems."

The students are puzzled and woozy. They require a metaphor.

"It's like being on a boat," the time travelers say. "How many of you have been on a boat?"

Some of the students raise their hands proudly. Some weakly. Some barf into their laps.

"Sometimes people get sick on boats," the time travelers explain. "While walking on the deck of a ship, their eyes tell their brains that the ground beneath them is level and stable, while their inner ears tell them that it isn't. For a while, the brains can't make sense of this. The brains know that things are not behaving as they should, which makes the brains uneasy, which makes the bodies uneasy. In time, a compromise is reached between the two senses, which allows for stable movement and surer footing. Sailors call this getting your sea legs."

The more the time travelers talk about the ocean, the greener the green students get. One spews anew at the word "legs." The time travelers with the buckets miss the burst, but catch the runoff.

"Something similar happens when you get too close to the time travel device, except the conflicting reports are coming at you in four dimensions instead of three. Everything should sort itself out after a few minutes. We call this getting your time legs." The time travelers' hopeful smiles are met with pinched noses, bloodshot eyes, and the spittle-laden breathing of the miserably ill.

"Does this still happen to you?" the sick students want to know.

"Occasionally," the time travelers say, replacing full buckets with empty ones. "Less than when we started."

There is a chime of tinkling sounds from the back of the conference room, as what was once an eighteenth-century

captain's sextant falls to the floor in a drizzle of geometri-
cally perfect golden pieces.

"Oops," the back-of-the-room students say.

"Oh God," say the time travelers.

"We're sorry," insist the back-of-the-roomers, fingers still
hanging in midair where the sextant used to be. To their
credit, they do look sincerely sorry. It's a look they produce
too quickly and too easily. The time travelers formerly on
vomit detail begin collecting fallen pieces of sextant.

"Can you fix it?" the students ask.

The time travelers answer: "No."

"Not even with your time machine?"

The time travelers answer: "No."

"Really?" ask the students.

The answer is: "Really."

"Why not?" the students want to know. "What's the point
of having a time machine if you can't use it to go back and
fix things?"

"Because," the time travelers explain, "time travel is expensive."

Which is half true. The whole truth is: Time travel is *extremely* expensive. The dedicated reactor used to power the
time travel device does not, strictly speaking, produce energy through the burning of actual money, but the joke often
made at the administrative level is: It might as well. In fact,
this field trip is the first step in a new PR strategy designed
to keep the Time Travel Institute afloat, since, at the moment, the institute is not, strictly speaking, floating.

Still, the time travelers are men and women of principle,

211

and even if such temporal manipulations, like, for instance, the rescuing of a priceless artifact from disassembly, or the preservation of a species from extinction, or the exploitation of the many lucrative possibilities of time travel that might keep a time travel institute financially solvent were possible—and they are—the time travelers would still never permit it. Which is exactly what they tell the students.

"And even if it wasn't expensive," they say, "we would still never permit it."

The students want to know: "Why not?"

The time travelers explain: "Because we're in the business of observing history, not changing it. Changing the past could have dire repercussions on the present. Imagine if someone went into the past and—"

"We get causality," the students interrupt. "We know H. G. Wells. We've seen *Back to the Future*."

"You've read H. G. Wells?"

"We watched a film adaptation of *The Time Machine* in science class."

Film adaptation or not, this pleases the time travelers. For the first time today, it feels as though the students do, in fact, have some appreciation for their work. Perhaps they should have opened with *Back to the Future*.

"We tend to prefer more scientifically rigorous source material," they lie, "but that's the general idea, yes."

"Are there other problems with time travel?" the front-of-the-roomers want to know.

"What do you mean?"

"Like, what about the observer effect?"

The time travelers are suddenly taken aback. Who has planted these ideas in the students' heads? Their enigmatic teacher, perhaps? Where *is* this person? The time travelers are preparing to offer this person a piece of their minds.

"Are you referring to the idea that the simple act of observing affects what is observed?" the time travelers ask. "Do you mean to imply that by objectively recording the past, we are, against our own best efforts, altering the outcome of events and doing irreparable harm to the fabric of history? Is that it?"

"That," say the front-of-the-roomers, "is basically what we're getting at, yeah." They are smiling. Their small butts twist in their chairs. Their heads bob like little balls of innocence.

"We can assure you," say the time travelers, "that is not the case."

"How can you be certain?" the students want to know.

"We are extremely careful."

"But if you did alter events, there'd be no way to know, because—"

"We don't alter events," say the time travelers.

"But you can't—"

"We don't alter events." They are adamant. "We know we don't because we don't. We have procedures and protocols and manuals. We've been doing this for a long time."

"Are you saying that the ethical dictums of your work have kept perfect pace with the moral dilemmas inherent to your technology?" the students ask.

"Maybe you don't want to see the time travel device after

all," the time travelers say. "Maybe you'd rather stay here and lecture us on how to do our jobs."

"Um, hey—" say the students.

"Or maybe you'd like to go climb around in the lobby for another hour or two. Or, *or*, maybe you'd like the adult assigned to your care to take you home. How about that? Do you even *have* an adult assigned to your care? That's what we'd like to know."

"Hey," the students say.

"What?" the time travelers snap.

"Some of us are older."

"What?"

"Some of us are older."

The time travelers ask: "What do you mean?"

The students mean: "Some of us are older than we were a few minutes ago. A handful of us look almost twenty. Is that normal?"

It's true. Some of the students now look a little too old to be in the third grade. Many of the students' clothes have tightened around them. Buttons have burst. The cheeks and chins of a handful of the boys have darkened. Some of the girls have begun playfully poking at their newly inflated chests. The students who have not grown stare wide-eyed at the students who have, vibrating with jealousy.

"Why aren't we growing?" they want to know.

The time travelers do not answer right away. They crowd around the stubbled chin of a male student for a closer examination. The hair looks real enough. Their staring makes the aging students nervous, and the nonaging students even more jealous.

"Why do they get to grow?" demand the still-young students.

"Is this because we don't have our time legs yet?" ask the young men and women who were once third graders, surprised by their own voices. They grasp at their throats. Clearing them changes nothing.

"No," the time travelers reply, "something's wrong. We need to check the time travel device."

With this, most of the time travelers hurry out of the room. The children who are still children are standing on their chairs, beating their fists against the conference table, demanding to grow up.

"Everyone, calm down," the remaining time travelers say. "No one else is going to grow up." And for the moment, no one does.

This comes as a relief to the remaining time travelers, who are a different breed than the rest. This particular group doesn't actually do a lot of time travel per se. They're mainly historical scholars and theorists charged with making sure that the Time Travel Institute's reference materials and field guides are as accurate as possible, and are rarely involved in the practical applications of their research. Some aren't even especially clear on how the time travel device actually works. They are desk jockey time travelers, masters of spreadsheets, filing codes, and the occasional odd job. At the moment, they're on vomit duty, and none of them is eager to be promoted to the role of conference leader. Mostly they just want to dab at puke stains and guard the remaining artifacts until the other time travelers return, allowing them to get back to their paperwork, which rarely throws up or breaks priceless antiquities. In the meantime, the desk jockey time travelers do their best to ignore the sick students, who are still feeling sick, and the aged students, who are quietly slipping under the conference table, and the back-of-the-room students, who are admiring the antique cutlasses a little too closely. They keep their eyes on their work. They're not the sort to get involved.

Under the conference table, the grown children wait for a cure to their adulthood. Their child-size clothing is comically tight around their new, long bodies, forcing sleeves and shirttails to be repeatedly tugged back into place. There isn't enough fabric to cover all the new skin, and trying only makes matters worse, as their now-adult brains, swimming in an acid bath of new hormones and chemicals, fire off unvetted commands that cannot possibly be followed (can they?) and desires too outrageous to be taken seriously (right?). "You first" is the standing dare, but no one dares. The grown students know they shouldn't be here, that they've arrived too early. And yet, here it is, the future, close enough to reach out and touch.

Then things get worse.

The desk jockey time travelers start to age. Rapidly. Their skin crinkles around their skulls like burned newspaper. Their tendons go slack as their muscles flash-atrophy. Their withering spines bow their heads closer to the floor. They're losing their teeth, their hair, the shapes of their faces. They sputter the last syllables of air out of their lungs like empty shampoo bottles. They pull their jumpsuits tighter around them, trying to hold everything together before collapsing to the floor, cataracts clouding their vision, ears suddenly deaf to the sound of children moaning in pain, and screaming in horror, and playing at war. There is a clanging of swords too heavy for the hands that hold them, the bursting of mouth-made rifle reports, the heavy *thunk* of feigned death. All at once the conference room reeks of sweat, and retch, and the curdled smell of the suddenly old.

Meanwhile, the now totally unmonitored back-of-the-room students, having skirmished their way through the entirety of the low-hanging arsenal, the British cavalry sabers and German Mausers and Confederate bayonets, turn their attention now toward an enormous silver blunderbuss hanging between a pair of Kentucky dueling pistols. They salivate at its stained cherrywood stock, its poised action pin cocked tight and big as a gorilla thumb, its iron thick as a church bell. It aches to be held, and the back-of-the-roomers want nothing more than to hold it, to feel its awesome historical weight in their arms, to point it at loyal friends and shout *bang*. The blunderbuss smiles down at them as they stack and swivel chairs, sighing as they balance on teetering armrests to reach it. They bear it over their heads like a golden calf, one that will snort, and stamp, and promise to break for them in every profound and potent way a thing can.

Then more things happen: One of the dying time travelers grows suddenly young again, yanked back in time on a rip cord until he is a toddler lost in the folds of his own gray jumpsuit. The same happens to the student carrying the blunderbuss, who's reduced to infancy so fast she's nearly flattened under the weight of the massive weapon. Without anyone noticing, the eighteenth-century captain's sextant is once again on its pedestal, completely restored, having returned to a time when it existed in one piece. Then, with a massive, oaken groan, the conference table is once again an ancient sequoia, strong and leafy. Its thick roots snake down into the carpet, pinning a tangle of half-naked men and women to the ground and punching through the ceiling of the conference room in a burst of untamable branches. The hail of ceiling tile is accompanied by the pitching of shouts and screams, the splintering of wooden pedestals, and an ominous, steady thump from the lobby growing louder and louder, until the wall of the room collapses, pummeled by a massive spiked tail. The roar of what is now a living stego-saurus rattles the remaining walls before a sweep of spines reduces them to rubble. Its enormous legs smithereen the room as bits of lunar rover dislodge from its dorsal spines. The only figures not cowering in pain or terror are the now fully armed back-of-the-room students, who in a few brave seconds prepare to make war with the massive beast. They raise their cutlasses and muskets, their axes and halberds. The blunderbuss suddenly grows younger in the hands of its carriers, returning to one of a thousand battles when it was loaded for bear. Its wick glows to life, its bell ready to breathe fire and belch shot, to shatter or be shattered, but all of this only for a moment, one tiny hiccup in time's otherwise smooth digestion, and then the moment passes, and the stegosaurus is once again a pile of bones, and the tree is a conference table, and the students and time travelers are younger and older in whatever direction returns them to the way they had been before their hold on the present deserted them.

The time travelers who had left earlier reenter the conference room, which is now a tragedy of priceless historical debris. They're wiping milky fluid off their hands and cheeks with large gray towels. Their jumpsuits are singed and burned away in places. Their hair is smoking. Their eyebrows are missing.

"The time travel device was leaking," they report. "We fixed it."

The returning time travelers check on everyone, beginning not with the students but with their colleagues, the desk jockey time travelers, who are huddled together, wailing louder and harder than any child.

Everyone decides the field trip is over. A school bus is summoned. The driver carries a license with dates of birth and expiration. He loads up the students, whose heads are still abuzz, some with visions of living dinosaurs, some with war, some with their first narcotic taste of other human bodies. They will not unbuzz for days. As the bus pulls away, they do not look back, or even think to wave good-bye.

The time travelers take the rest of the day off. They retire to the Time Travel Institute's residential wing to nap and watch television, but cannot truly relax. They are thinking about the wrecked and mangled artifacts on the conference room floor, many of which had been taken directly from the field. It turns out that the ethical dictums of their work have not, in fact, kept perfect pace with the moral dilemmas inherent to their technology. Each has pocketed a souvenir in his or her travels. Or two. They know that they shouldn't have taken, shouldn't have touched, but the time travelers, for all their virtue and rigor, are still human. They filled a conference room with objects they presumed no one in history would miss. But the students—and this makes them so angry—the students are right: There's no way to know for sure. It's possible, they admit to themselves now, that they've been tugging at threads that shouldn't be tugged. A broken time travel device is one thing, but a broken history . . .

Slipping into their pajamas, they try to shake off the sneaking suspicion that their procedures and protocols and manuals haven't protected anything, that their whole enterprise is fatally flawed, that, in the end, they're only making things worse. As they brush their teeth, they worry about causality, and the observer effect, and the very real possibility of accidentally erasing someone from history. Someone like themselves.

All time travelers share the same secret fear: that one day their collective lack of self-control, their inability to resist looking, touching, taking, will purge them from the ranks of having ever existed, robbing them of a life, a death, and a birth all at once. Honestly, when they really think about it, it's a miracle it hasn't happened already.

These are the thoughts that keep time travelers up at night.

"Will you make sure that I'm not erased?" they ask again

as they tuck one another into bed. "Will you make sure that I'm born? That I live when I'm supposed to? That I die when the time is right?"

"We will," the time travelers hush, turning out the light. "We will."

Acknowledgments

Everything is impossible. And then it isn't. When this happens, there are usually people to thank.

Sword-and-shield thanks to my unstoppable agent PJ Mark (stop him, just you try it), whose laser-beam readings and raw hustle are just two talents in a quiver of many. Thanks also to Ian Bonaparte and Marya Spence for their sharp eyes and sharper suggestions.

Whip-smart thanks to the great Maya Ziv, editor extraordinaire, who just makes everything better (sentences, scenes, brief swings through New York), and whose radiant enthusiasm carried me through much of this book. Thanks also to Ben Sevier, Christine Ball, Maddy Newquist, Wendy Pearl, and everyone else at Dutton for their kindness and support.

Spotlight thanks to Willing Davidson, Michael Ray, Claire Boyle, and Emma Komlos-Hrobsky for helping some of these stories thrive outside their natural habitat.

Sage thanks to my incredible teachers: When Geoffrey Wolff admires one of your sentences, you feel like a goddamn superhero. When Brad Watson listens to what stories

ACKNOWLEDGMENTS

are saying, you feel like you've been deaf to them your whole life. Maile Meloy will show you that even the ridiculous should be taken seriously. When Ron Carlson talks shop, you remember why you love writing, and writers. When C. J. Hribal encourages you, there's a good chance it'll change your life. David and Phylis Ravel will teach you that loving deeply is the artist's greatest calling. And when Michelle Latiolais invites you over for lunch, once again lending her brilliant insight to your work and her calm counsel to your fears, you'll invariably leave with a lighter heart, a resuscitated courage, and what's left of the chocolate cake.

Vanguard thanks to that gang of literary thugs I am most eager to please: Ramona Ausubel, Marisa Matarazzo, and Matt Sumell, who demanded many of these stories into being. Be ever whole and ever true, our little coterie.

Roundtable thanks to Lauren Coleman, Izzy Prcic, Max Winter, Michelle Chihara, Dave Morris, Erin Almond, Kevin Lee, Zach Braun, Frank D'Amato, and all the other great UCI writers for seeing me through those earliest of early days.

Rescue-team thanks to Cristina Rodriguez and Leila Mansouri for emergency readings both keen and clutch. Thanks for hearing me out, talking me down, and pointing out what was right under my nose. And to Amanda Foushee, for regularly knocking sense into my sometimes senseless head.

Home-team thanks to the UCI School of Humanities and the International Center for Writing and Translation for the grants; and to Ann Heine for her support and the support she continues to give young writers.

ACKNOWLEDGMENTS

And finally, alpha-and-omega thanks to my family: Tom, Tiffany, Beth, Andy, Karen, Andrew, and Megan, and to the greatest of all parents, John and Mary Eileen. Thank you for giving me the freedom I desperately needed, the patience I didn't deserve, and the stalwart, selfless love that astonishes me still. I love you deeper than sea, wider than sky.